A Different Harbor

A Different Harbor

Stories by
Elizabeth Genovise

Mayapple Press 2014

Published by   MAYAPPLE PRESS
                 362 Chestnut Hill Rd.
                 Woodstock, NY 12498
                 www.mayapplepress.com

ISBN 978-1-936419-38-8
Library of Congress Control Number: 2014935314

ACKNOWLEDGMENTS

Cold Mountain Review: A Different Harbor
The Pinch: Transmissions
The Southern Review: The Seiche
Yemassee: Burl Wood

I owe the deepest gratitude to my teachers, Neil Connelly, John Somerville, and Inge Boss, whose labors of love have shaped the arc of my life. I want to thank my family—Mom, Dad, Frank, and Chris—for their support and for their stories. Finally, I am indebted to my longtime friend and reader, Kate Klein, and to the members of my MFA workshop back at McNeese State University, for the wisdom and encouragement they have shared with me over the years.

Cover design by Judith Kerman. Cover photo from Rundesroom.com used under Creative Commons, modified by inclusion of a trilobite fossil. Book designed and typeset by Amee Schmidt with titles in Oregon LDO Medium and text in Californian FB. Author photo courtesy of Chris Hodges.

Contents

The Seiche   3

Burl Wood   17

On the French Coast   37

Transmissions   51

A Different Harbor   61

For my brother

The Seiche

I love mornings in this house, the stolid brightness of them. Even at this time of year, when autumn has given way to winter, pale blue sun rays bounce off the surface of Lake Michigan and at nine o'clock reach exactly halfway across the kitchen floor. When the light filters through the Stanleys' handmade curtains, it forms hieroglyphics across the tile, rounded and intricate. By the time I'm done brewing tea, the letters on the floor have scattered, replaced with the late-morning chatter of one or both of the Stanleys.

They always have plenty to talk about. Frank Stanley, seventy-six years old, used to be a merchant seaman. His wife Adele is two years younger and taught history until she was sixty. Both speak several languages and have seen ten or twelve countries of the world. They read science magazines, plant gardens full of exotic things, translate poetry. But they are dying, and that's the reason I'm here: they put an ad out two years ago, looking for a "fresh and energetic person to assist with housekeeping, cooking and caretaking," and there I was, reading the ad while sitting on my bed at the Motel 6 in Traverse City, just a few miles from where the two of them lived.

During my first week living with them, Adele told me that she and Frank had been given a few months to live. Cancer, of course, she'd said. But the months came and went and I came to disbelieve the doctors entirely.

3

I couldn't leave, though. The two of them have fascinated me from the day I moved in. Their house, settled back from the city amidst the endless vineyards along Lake Michigan, was enough to cement me in place after that first week. Lining their shelves and mantles are bottles of shells from countless beaches, colored fans and pottery bowls, things Frank had picked up in ports all over the world when he was young.

The best is the living room, where Frank built a shelf encircling all four walls at about eye level. Beginning just to the left of the door, and going all the way around to the right of it, is a line of picture frames, each frame filled with a thick collage of dried leaves. The leaves, Adele explained to me, were from each autumn of their life together, beginning with their first year. That was why the frames on the left side of the door held the palest leaves, while the leaves at the end of the line were brightest. The first time I was alone in that room, I counted the frames to make sure there really was one for every year. When I asked Adele about the scattered three that were missing, she said, "Those weren't banner years," but it seems more likely that the frames just got lost in the shuffle. This isn't the first house they've lived in.

Today is Thanksgiving—my second one with the Stanleys—and I love how the holidays in this house come without tension, without any anxiety about mealtimes or surprises or places to go. We treat these days like any others. The only difference is that Frank and Adele save their best stories for the holidays, and I look forward to that, the doors that open during times like this.

I brew the tea. Through the kitchen window I watch the newly-stripped trees, brittle and still, and I look past them at the Lake. The waters on our end of the bay are shallow, but they haven't frozen yet. Nothing is moving out there but the waves.

When the phone rings, I drop the cup I'm holding and luckily it lands in a wicker basket full of knickknacks instead of on the kitchen floor. I lunge for the phone and grab it before the second ring. The ringer is as loud as a smoke alarm, and Frank and Adele will be wanting at least another hour of sleep.

"Hello?" I say. I hold the phone a little away from my ear, listening for sounds from the Stanleys' bedroom, but all is quiet.

"Maggie? Hello? It's Laurel . . . Are you there?"

"I'm here," I say. I cross the kitchen to the opposite window, stretching out the phone cord, and peer out into the backyard. Adele had me rake the leaves yesterday, and the two stuffed bags look precarious, leaning against the shed.

"Is this a bad time?"

"You do realize it's Thanksgiving today. And kind of early."

"Oh, I know. I know. This isn't just about White Arrow now, though."

I suppress a sigh. Crammed under my mattress is a thick information packet from the White Arrow Academy in Tennessee—a packet I hid when it first came in the mail. Laurel, once my roommate of two semesters back in college, started the school after graduation, and has been calling since August to recruit me. I don't know why she picked me, of all people—she and I have barely spoken since my divorce, and we weren't the best of friends in school either.

It baffles me that she keeps trying. I've told her that I have a job, that I'm happy with it. And I've made it pretty clear that I'm not waiting breathlessly for a position in her Tennessee schoolhouse. I've never even seen the state. I can't imagine myself there.

"Maggie? Are you burning something on the stove, or what?"

"No."

"Well—all right. Really I just wanted to call and wish you a happy Thanksgiving, that's all. It must be beautiful up there. If it's half as beautiful as it is here. You haven't seen what November can really look like until you've seen it in the hills, you know."

I stare at the ceiling. I can't picture this, these enormous hills she's described to me before. I see sand dunes sprouting pines and then my mind goes blank. Still, I listen as she goes on, talking about Cumberland and the river behind the school, how cold it's gotten, how the old waterwheel is back to working again. Her accent back at school used to unnerve me and it still does, because I have to listen so hard to catch certain words. But it's beautiful sometimes, like when *windows* becomes *wind doves* and *held* becomes *hailed*.

"The real crazy thing," she says, "is how the leaves all turn blue and purple after the first snow."

I blink, and say, "What?"

There is a pause, and then Laurel's laugh, like a rush of warm water, breaks the silence. "That was a test," she says.

"I was listening, really. I was."

"Okay," she says. Then, "Listen, Maggie. I'm not sure the right way to say this."

I start twisting the phone cord into knots.

"We're making our final selections for next semester. And a lot of these people coming in are probably going to stay for awhile. Know what I mean?"

"Yes."

"So I'm saying that you need to—to make your decision. You've had a lot of time. I know this is difficult for you, but you have to believe me when I tell you that I want you here. You're made for this place. It's in every word of what we have on you. I—we—would be lucky to have you. And so would our kids."

I pull one of Adele's embroidered towels off the counter and trace its pattern with my forefinger. I say nothing. I never speak when Laurel talks like this.

"Maggie."

"I'm here."

"Could I call you tonight, maybe? Talk this over some more later?"

"Don't you have family?" I say. I hear myself and immediately say, "I'm sorry, that came out—"

"Yeah, Maggie, I do. This is my hometown, remember?" For the first time, her soft voice takes on an edge.

"I know that. Of course I know that. I'm sorry," I say. "I don't know if I'll be here tonight, though. I'm not sure."

"You won't be at home tonight? For Thanksgiving?"

"I don't know."

"Well." There is a pause. "Either way . . . I'll talk to you soon."

"All right."

I put the phone back in its cradle and when I look up, Adele is in the doorway, holding onto its frame for support. "Laurel?" she says.

I shrug. "Laurel. Did I wake you?"

She ignores my question. "So who *is* she, already? Who is this young lady? The last time she called and I answered it, she was so darling on the phone."

"A friend from school," I say. "Nobody important."

Adele narrows her eyes at me. "Like fish."

6

I laugh. "I can't take you seriously when you use that phrase." I watch as she lowers herself into a chair at the table. "I was going to make bread," I say. "Will you eat it tonight, if I do?"

"Of course. Frank won't, but I will."

Adele and I sink into a comfortable quiet as I work. This, too, is part of our mornings: a soft pillowed silence now and then, where we are aware of each other's thinking but not each other's thoughts. It is always Adele who begins a conversation, and when I've started with the dough, she leans forward across the table and says, "Have you ever really thought how depressing it is, that things take mold like that, but the shape doesn't last? The way water fills a bowl but gives meaning to the shape only until you tilt it, or pour it out."

"Why do you always have to make me think in the morning?" It's our standard joke.

"Because I know you were already thinking anyway." She opens the refrigerator and starts rearranging things, changing the way I have aligned them. There is a pause. Then she says, "Do you know that for the first few years while Frank was away at sea, I almost left him? I nearly did. There wasn't anybody else. But I couldn't take it anymore, feeling like every time we made something, it lost its shape because he wasn't there to help me keep its angles. You know what I mean?"

I think, *and the doors fly open.* "You never would have left him," I say firmly. Her declaration shakes me, though, once it settles in. It surprises me to see my fingers trembling a little over the dough.

"Oh yes I would have. I have that cruelty in me. You don't believe it?"

I look at her, bent and tiny, now sorting through the preserve jars on the second shelf. "Nope. I don't."

"That," Adele says matter-of-factly, "is because you don't have any in you."

I laugh, but Adele is quiet. After a moment she says into the fridge, "I'm betting that *he* did, though, didn't he? Maybe you wouldn't like me so much if you knew how much like him I probably was at your age."

I don't even bother to ask, "Who?" She is talking about John, my ex-husband. Really, all she knows about him is that he left me, but she has a way of telling me about myself and my life to make up for my own silences.

I say, "Maybe he left because I was cruel."

Adele turns around and shakes her head at me. "I hate to tell you, but it's unimaginable. You're too much like Frank, and I know Frank. No cruelty."

I set the bread in the oven and Adele sits back down. "Frank is a very deep paradox," she says. "He has loved movement all his life, can't stay in one place. But he has to preserve all his moments under glass. He saves everything. He's worse than a pack rat."

"I know."

"I used to get so irritated. I would even throw things out behind his back. I thought he was ridiculous. Childish."

I don't say anything but go to reheat the tea. I reach for the sugar bowl and then remind myself, as I do almost every day, that nobody in this house takes sugar in their tea.

Adele says, "Once he filled a suitcase full of things from a port way out in the Orient and it got lost on its way back here. He insured it and everything, but it got lost, and when he found out he'd never get the case back, it was like someone had died. He was hysterical. I couldn't believe it."

"Maybe he felt like that because he moved so much," I say. "Maybe everything felt just a little too flimsy to him. I don't know."

"That's the girl I love," Adele says softly. She puts her chin in her hand and fixes her pale eyes on me as I pour the tea. "You have a knack for finishing the thoughts I haven't gotten around to finishing."

"Hardly."

There's a soft squeak in the living room—Frank's wheelchair on the hardwood floor—and then Frank rolls in, using his feet to propel himself forward. He is groggy in his dark blue pajamas. Grinning, he shakes one of his lean brown fingers at us. "Women alone together in a kitchen, there is nothing deadlier. What have you two been talking about this time?"

Adele hands him a cup of the tea. "You."

Frank sighs and rolls his eyes heavenward. He has a flair for the dramatic. I say, "Which port story will you tell over dinner tonight? Make it good. Preferably one with a man-eating shark, or a shipwreck."

"Shipwreck," Adele mutters. "Closest he ever got to one was on Lake Superior, right in the harbor. Bumped into another boat. Like a fender-bender on water."

I laugh a little and wait for Frank's inevitable sarcasm. But he surprises me, his eyes suddenly lighting up. "I do have a good story," he says. "About Lake Superior. I haven't told you this one, Maggie." He looks over at Adele. "The seiche?"

She cocks her head, considering, and then nods at Frank over her tea. "Yes. That is a good one."

"It's a good time for it," Frank says. "The perfect time."

We eat at five, making a crowded corner at one end of their big dining room table, and we eat slowly and in silence. There's always a lull before Frank talks, just like with Adele, and it's after six when I stand up and begin clearing away the dishes. I leave the centerpiece, a cobalt vase filled with bright paper flowers. Adele lights candles and spreads them out across the table. When I finish clearing the food, I bring a blanket back with me and wrap it around Adele's shoulders before I sit down again.

I watch as Frank and Adele finish their coffee in small sips. The evening sun streams in through the dining room window and flushes across their faces so that they look younger, healthier. In my head I say a crazy little prayer that they will live forever, and then look around, embarrassed, as if they've heard me.

Frank leans forward in his wheelchair, setting down his mug. "This story," he says, grinning crookedly, "is not about a port."

"Evasion," I say. I arrange myself cross-legged in my chair, getting comfortable. "But I'll accept it."

The phone rings and I jump. Adele looks pointedly at me.

"I'm not getting it," I say. But the ring is distressingly loud and I have to resist actually clapping my hands over my ears.

"Maggie," Adele says. "For heaven's sake just answer it. It's Laurel, isn't it?"

"Let it ring," I say. "It's not her, and even if it were, there's no reason to get up and answer it during Thanksgiving dinner, don't you think? Don't you think it's a little rude to call at this hour?"

It rings a fourth time and then quiets. Adele shakes her head and seems ready to say something, but Frank comes to my rescue by loudly clearing his throat. "So it's not about a port," he says. "But. You'll like this one better."

"Perfect."

I settle back in my chair, trying to relax, and Frank and Adele lean back, too, remembering.

If they had it right, Frank had been about twenty-four at the time. He had just taken a job carrying minerals across Lake Superior to Copper Harbor, and it was a beautiful part of the Lake that he got to stay on, up on the Keweenaw Peninsula where at night the water mirrored the stars and the Estivant pines looked like black castles against the sky. Adele, tired of being left in Traverse Bay where they'd grown up together, pleaded with him to find her a place to stay out there until he was through with the job. What Frank found was a house that was once a bed-and-breakfast, a knotty-pine-walled place with three floors and a twisting staircase. The woman who lived there was letting out the rooms, and Frank had Adele placed in the den on the third floor: a bizarre world of its own, a sailor's room, with iron anchors mounted to the wall and windows covered in stained glass oddities.

In the weeks before Adele's coming, Frank had gotten to know the old woman, Marta, who owned the house, and she was an eccentric, telling stories of her dead husband (also a waterman) over and over again. Marta's stories never bothered Frank until the day she told him that she firmly believed there was a shipwreck, or the remains of one, just beyond the first dropoff in the patch of lake behind the house.

She told him she didn't know what, exactly, was down there, and that made it worse, because Frank had always had a wild imagination, and in his mind he saw skeletons: bones of the ship itself, bones of men. On the train back, he could not stop seeing silver-green water eroding the bones, and Adele, who loved to swim, passing over the dropoff and seeing those things in the depths. He thought it was a bad omen, and he could not get it out of his mind.

So halfway to Traverse Bay he changed trains and went back to the Upper Peninsula. He talked it over with Marta and then he had boundary ropes, with a buoy marking the northeast corner, strung out in a wide square on the lake behind the house. The dropoff was safely beyond the strings, invisible. This space in the shallows, he told Marta, was where Adele should swim or wade if she wanted to go into the water. It would be safer, he told her. Before he left again, he stood alone on the beach at twilight, staring out at the glittering blue square and the bright lilting buoy, with the red and violet horizon beyond its borders.

Within the week, Adele moved into the little room at Marta's, knowing nothing about what Frank had done with the beach. And she swam, as he'd predicted, braving the water that was frigid even during that June, while Frank ferried minerals back and forth across the lake.

One clear July night, the two women stood on the dock behind the house and watched the Northern Lights, green and yellow waves bearing stars like floating sand dollars, until very late. Marta was talking a good deal, telling Adele all about her husband, and then it just came out: first, the rumor about the shipwreck, and then, what Frank had done before he brought Adele up to the peninsula.

Adele was furious for what seemed like the hundredth time that summer. In bed that night, looking at the sailor's anchors hung on the wall, she'd wondered: what was Frank so afraid of? That she'd see the wreck, and in seeing it, would bring down all manner of disasters upon the two of them? She knew Frank, even when they were so young, knew what he was seeing: the wreck and the two of them in a twisted embrace, their perfection ruined.

Frank was at sea that night, but the following day when he came back to the house, Adele told him just what she thought. She said, "Things die, Frank. And ropes and a buoy aren't going to keep that back from us. Accept it and stop this." When he was silent, sullen, she went up to her room in Marta's house and closed the door on him. So Frank went back to work in a storm, thinking she might leave him, and in his way, thinking that he'd been right all along: there'd been a wreck.

"The thing he'd always been afraid of," Adele says, shaking her head and pulling the blanket tighter around her shoulders. "A wreck."

I imagine what Frank must have seen in his mind then. A shattered hull, a ragged helm, a mast lying on the lake floor like the spine of some creature long dead. A double bed with a single pillow. A train ticket for one.

"Are you even listening?" Frank raises one eyebrow at me. "You know us. We like a captive audience."

"I'm listening," I say. "I promise. Go on."

So after Frank left that day, Adele decided to go for a swim, an act of rebellion. And that happened to be the day of one of the most sudden and dramatic seiches on Lake Superior: a nine-foot shift in water level that sent all the boats in the harbors thumping against each other, way on the other end of the lake where Frank was.

Adele was in the water when the seiche came, and it came fast. Within minutes the water had rushed away from the shore and exposed the dropoff. The buoy and its ropes went limp, and Adele, standing now in absolute astonishment on the soaked and rocky lake floor, moved slowly down to the bared edge and looked over.

There was no shipwreck. Instead the lake floor teemed with life. The coppery bottom sparkled in the sun, and tiny scuttling creatures, suddenly ousted from their homes, rushed downward toward the receding waterline. Adele reached down and brought up a rich handful of the sand. Even as she stared into the grains, the water began to filter back into the hollow. She stayed where she was. She watched the water rise up along her legs and stomach; she was so lost in the feeling of it that it shocked her when the water wet her lips, threatened to cover her nose. Adele pushed herself up off the sandy floor and began swimming again. And then, almost as quickly as it had come, the seiche was finished.

"I didn't get to see what she saw," Frank says, closing his eyes for a minute as if trying to. "I wish I had."

"Of course," Adele sighs, "he was upset that I didn't keep that handful of sand. As if I could hold onto it while I was swimming. But he did go back and get the darned buoy itself, which is now buried in our attic."

I laugh, and they join in. So often I go to bed thinking, *this solitude in another, there is no end to it.* I'll stay up half the night feeling this hollow ache like I haven't eaten in days. But after nights like these, I feel blanketed in their memories, and I can sleep.

When our laughter has petered out, there is a long silence. Frank snuffs out the candles and Adele sits with her chin on her hands, covering her lips with her fingers.

"Well," I say at last. "Should we turn in?"

"Not quite yet," Adele says, eyes drifting to Frank's. "Frank and I have to do something first, while the sun's not quite gone."

"What is it?"

They both look at me, and it dawns on me that there is something like pity in their expressions. "You might not like to be there and watch," Frank says after a hesitation. "It might be—I don't know."

"No," Adele says. She shakes her head at Frank. "She should."

I look back and forth between them. "What? What's going on?"

"Maggie." Adele's voice is so gentle, so solemn, that I sit bolt upright.

"What?" I say again. Another silence settles on us, but this time it feels different. I wait for Adele to say something and I start worrying the fabric of my chair cushion with my nails.

"Maggie," she says at last. "We're dying. We're on our way. You need to understand that."

I stare at her. "You've lived past every date they've given you," I say, a little shrilly. Panic is creeping up my throat. "Where is this coming from all of a sudden? You're healthy. It's incredible how strong you both are. Why are you—"

"We're not." She reaches over and wraps her hand around my wrist. "It's all right, Maggie. You've been so good to us. You've done everything there is to do, everything you could. But what's happening is happening, and I don't want any of us, least of all you, to pretend something different." She glances at Frank. "You've done everything there is to do," she says again.

I reach across the table with my free hand and nudge the centerpiece toward me. I rub a smear off the base and then push the vase away when I see my own reflection in the glass. "You're telling me to leave?"

Her hand stays on my arm but she doesn't respond. I turn toward Frank, but his gaze is on the tabletop.

"The two of us, we have something to do," Adele says at last. She withdraws her hand, and I look down at my wrist. "You should come outside with us."

I say nothing. I hear a small sigh slip from Adele before she gets up and goes over to Frank. Wordlessly she guides him out of the dining room, down the hallway to the living room, and then I hear what sounds like things being dropped into a box. I stay where I am, listening, until I hear the back door open. Then I cross over to the kitchen window and look out.

I watch as Adele wheels Frank onto the grass and then drags over the yard bags by the shed. She overturns them, letting the leaves I raked spill out into a coppery circle on the lawn. She goes briefly back into the house, and when she returns, she is dragging a cardboard box behind her. Together they reach into the box and start pulling out wooden picture frames. Their leaves.

One at a time, they pull the backs off the frames and then let the leaves tumble out into the pile. Rose, palest brown, dusty yellow, black. Some of them lift in the wind, and the rest get lost in the first pile. I start forward, horrified; I wait for Frank to reach down and grab them, but he doesn't. The two of them just keep opening frames until there are none left. Then Adele helps Frank out of his wheelchair, and they kneel down with their backs to the pile. She puts her arm behind his back and they let themselves drop backward into the leaves. They lie still.

I close my eyes. I stay in my place against the window for a long time, frozen there. I find myself remembering my first night in this house, when the three of us went into the backyard with lemonade and Frank tried to make me comfortable by asking me a volley of questions. "Tell me about Chicago," he'd said. "Does the Lake look the same there? Tell me about your family." Then, trying a livelier tone, "Tell me about the best experience of your life so far." I hadn't answered his last question.

This is what I think of as the best experience of my life. Five years ago, on a night in autumn, John and I took the train into downtown Chicago and walked all through the city, completely losing track of the time. We missed the last train back. He had some friends out there, so we found their apartment building, a high-rise on the north side, and took an elevator to the thirtieth floor. We were given a pull-out sofa to sleep on, in a room poorly lit and opening onto a tiny balcony.

We hardly knew each other then; we had no understanding yet between us. But the moment we were alone in the dark, the sound of light traffic streaming in through the balcony doors, John reached for me and crushed me against him like it was our one and only chance in the world to hold each other. He kept my hand clasped in his all the way until morning. When we woke at dawn, we went out onto the balcony and watched Lake Michigan turn from blue to rose under a soft mist. We said to each other, *this is it, this is everything we could want.* And when John's friends offered us a ride back to the suburbs, John refused, saying we'd take a morning train back.

There was a fog over the city as we walked to the station. On Canal Street, as we drew close to the bridge, I saw a flush of scarlet across the planks and looked over at John. He smiled and pressed me forward. When we stepped through the fog I saw that the bridge was strewn with rose petals. They were everywhere, deep red and wet with dew, and when John laid one in my hands, it felt rich and wild with life. We stood there a long time, breathing in the scent, and I never asked where they had come from, because I knew it was him.

I still have that petal he handed me, locked in a frame of my own. And it breaks my heart that if he were to look at it now, he would see only a color, the bruise of violet on white, and nothing more.

All I've wanted is to stay here, where my memories are under glass and can't scatter. But I know that memory is a buoy, and a buoy doesn't travel, can't carry you back to shore or further out to sea. It is only a placeholder, reminding you of the waters you once swam in—waters that will have to deepen if you ever want to move again.

Burl Wood

When Cal comes downstairs, tangled up in his pajamas and looking for a glass of water, he finds his father asleep on the couch in front of a frozen screen. Cal has found him this way many times over the last few weeks, slumped in front of a stilled video, often with a half-dozen beer bottles scattered across the coffee table, but lately it's been the same video on repeat. He recognizes the still: it is Lake Superior, the shore rocky and copper-red where the sun hits it, and in mid-gesture on the right is his mother. Her hair is in its characteristic knot, her sailor's blouse mid-flutter. The video is from a trip they took four years ago, when Cal was six. His memory of it is hazy, a stream of sounds and colors; he remembers foghorns, and freezing cold water, and a shop that had rows and rows of glittering stones.

"Dad," he says.

"Uhh." His father sits up a little, then sinks back down. "What's the matter, Cal?"

"You left the TV on again."

"It's okay, bud, I'm not going to bed yet. Just leave it."

"You want some water, Dad?"

"No thanks, bud. No, wait. Yeah. I do."

Cal goes and gets the water, padding back into the living room with the two glasses brimming. His father sits all the way up and takes one, shaking his head. "I'm sorry. I don't know why I've been so tired lately."

Cal fishes around for a good response, one that doesn't mention his mother. "Well, it's your job. It's not an easy job."

His father laughs, a weak laugh that nonetheless sends some water sloshing out of his glass. "Oh kid, it's not really."

Cal's father works for Metra. He doesn't like to tell people that he is a conductor, since he rarely "drives the train," as he calls it. He spends more time walking up and down the cars, taking tickets and telling people to take their feet off the seats. He helps teenagers get their bikes onto the cars, helps usher people to empty cars during the weekday morning rush. He told Cal years ago that it was the only job he ever wanted, even in college, and that he didn't care if people believed him.

"Did anything happen today? Did you have to kick anybody off?" Cal asks.

"Um, not today. I almost did—this smart-aleck who always dangles his legs over the luggage rack. But I let it go. Sometimes it's just not worth it."

Cal nods.

"How was school? I didn't ask you when you came home."

"It was all right. Cory asked me if I wanted to go to camp with him in June."

"Oh yeah? That something you want to do?"

"Not really." Cal wipes at the condensation on his glass. "I'd rather stay here with you."

"Oh yeah?"

"Yeah."

His father reaches over, rubs at Cal's mess of dark hair. "Who says I need so much company?"

Cal doesn't answer, and they look at each other until Cal's father turns back to the television. "I was watching an old movie," he says.

"I know. I think I'm going back to bed, Dad. You want me to start it playing again?"

"No, it's okay. Goodnight, bud."

"'Night."

In the morning, something is different about the kitchen. Cal's father has gone to work, leaving Cal's lunch packed and ready as always, but something is different. Cal turns in a circle, tapping his chin. It is a game he played with his mother before she died, always in these last few minutes before the bus came: *What's different, Cal?* she'd ask, tapping her chin. He thought it was a little silly, knew he was getting too old for it, but he'd follow suit, turning this way and that, to figure out what minute thing she'd changed. One time she took the Gumby figurine off the windowsill and stuck him into the teapot; another time, she stuck a tiny flower into one of the eyelets in the sand dollar glued to the window. He always got it, sometimes at the exact moment the bus squealed up against the curb outside the house.

"A lot of things," he mutters now, kicking the recycling bin with its medley of beer cans and bottles. "Dad, you're out of it. You're like that poet who spent a whole day writing one word." It's something his mother often said to his father, a joke between them that Cal doesn't understand, but he likes the tone of it, likes that he can match his mother's way of saying it. He scans the windowsills, the stove, the top of the fridge. He finds it up there: a big serving bowl, blue and yellow with a picture of a trout painted onto its side. He recognizes it, though he hasn't seen it in what seems like forever.

He can remember his father laughing about it: "Liz, it's hideous."

His mother: "It's a souvenir! It's folk art."

"It's hideous."

Cal hears the bus outside, can practically smell it through the screen door, and without thinking he ducks back behind the refrigerator and stays there until he hears it drive off. He tiptoes into the living room, locks the front door. He has never skipped a day of school before. He turns around as if checking the room for spies, and then walks to the VCR. He pushes Play and sits down on the floor.

His father must have continued watching the video after he'd gone to bed, because it is in a different place now. Cal's mother, leading Cal by the hand and balancing a knapsack on her other arm, is standing on a dock, with the lake behind her. Cal can see a lighthouse draped in fog in the background. "Let's run a motel out here," his mother says, laughing. Her cheeks look sunburned. "Cal could be our receptionist."

His father's voice: "I don't see any railroads out here. And you know how cold it gets here in winter? It'd be a nightmare."

"Forget trains. You could fish! Let's get started immediately."

"Are you proposing we steal a boat?"

"*Make* us a boat, Brody," Cal's mother said. She laughed again and then crouched down to look Cal in the eyes. "What do you think, Cal?"

Cal's small voice: "I hate fish."

Leaning back on the heels of his hands, Cal laughs, and then stops, feeling guilty about the sound. He looks around. A clank on the porch makes his hair stand on end until he realizes it's just the mailman. He lets the video play on; it skips around in time, shifting to a moment in front of a small restaurant, then to their trip across the bay to the lighthouse from the first shot. Cal doesn't remember this part, but it doesn't matter; he watches his mother, listens for her. During the lighthouse tour, when his father is filming the tour guide's presentation, he can hear his mother in the background: "There's *writing* on these walls. It's children's writing." The tour guide stops his speech and says, "Oh, it's everywhere. We don't know which families they're all from. That kind of thing was a common occurrence, since they couldn't leave very often." Cal strains to hear his mother's response, but the tape doesn't pick it up. He freezes the screen as his father had done the night before, and moves up close to it on his knees. His face nearly to the glass, he tries to pick out the writing on the lighthouse walls, as his mother must have.

Brody has been fired. It is his third day without a job; he has been leaving the house to keep up appearances, but he has a feeling the whole town knows. He came aboard drunk last week, and that was that. Probably no one would have noticed what was wrong with him, had he not gotten into an absurd argument with a passenger who wanted change for a fifty-dollar bill. But then again, he could hardly hold himself up whenever the train stopped; he kept clutching at things, and when he looked up, someone would be staring at him, as if knowing.

It bothers him that after just three days off the job, he feels lost. It's the absence of the announcements, the rhythm of the cars, his own perfectly-timed step down off the platform to usher people on. All the parameters of his day are abruptly missing, and he catches himself looking around him during boarding-times, as though waiting for someone to step up beside him.

Burl Wood

Today he goes to the Elmhurst Public Library, avoiding Villa Park's library in hopes of lessening his chance of seeing someone he knows. He likes Elmhurst's library better anyway, with its tall windows, and its low shelves topped with aquariums containing things that kids liked to stop and look at, hermit crabs and frogs.

He hasn't had a drink this morning and resolves not to, but he eats his way through an entire package of mints, afraid someone will know what he's been doing up until today. With a librarian's help, he finds stacks of books on boat-building and spreads them out across a table in the far corner of the first floor reading area.

The books don't help. Most of them talk about shipbuilding, things on a scale Brody can't even comprehend. He feels ridiculous just looking at them. He wants some simple instructions for the smallest boat imaginable. A rowboat, a canoe, something he can take Cal out on, maybe on Herrick Lake, some small body of water where it would be safe. Brody pushes the books aside, muttering "service aisle" the way his father used to in restaurants, and gets up again. He nearly bowls the librarian over.

She is a tiny, elderly woman in a paisley skirt and blouse. "So they didn't work out?" she says.

"Not really. I'm looking for instructions to make something a little smaller."

"Oh. Ohh." She cocks her head. "You need some woodworking manuals, maybe. Start with the basics?"

He has a feeling she misunderstands, but he says, "Well, that might be more helpful."

She shows him the section, but when she leaves, Brody finds himself sitting on the thinly-carpeted floor with a book that's not about woodworking, but wood itself. It is a new book, glossy as an encyclopedia, and he marvels at the fact that he hasn't looked at any sort of picture book in years. He's immersed in poems and plays when he gets home at night. Maps and picture books were always Liz's province—astronomy, botany, things like that. Brody stops at the chapter called "Burl Species."

He leans back against the shelf behind him. The pictures are oddly fascinating—there is something otherworldly, almost three-dimensional, about the pattern of the grain on the slices of wood, and the colors are richly varied. He reads, *A burl is a kind of tumor that forms on a tree, usually near its base, as a result of one of several possible factors. The grain is without pattern, which makes the wood extremely dense and difficult to work with. If removed when the tree is still alive, the removal will destroy the tree, since the burl takes root in the tree's major artery. If removed after a certain stage in its growth, the burl will have lost its density and will have decayed from the inside out. Burls are highly sought-after by woodworking artists due to the rarity of their grain.*

There are pictures of the "factors" as well as of the burls—disease; green and white rot feathering out from tree trunks; insects in swarms; a flooded forest. Sudden changes in the tree's surroundings that spawn the burl's growth. Brody turns the page to a close-up of a slab of pine burl. The caption reads, *Burl wood, when removed at the proper time, has a density high enough to endure even the most severe circumstances without damage.* The wood looks alien to Brody, but he wouldn't have called it diseased; instead, it looks wild the way spots on a leopard do, or stones under a river. His eye can't quite follow the swirls of the grain, and eventually, he closes the book, his head aching. But he holds it in his hands, thinking.

Cal's friends Mark and Cory show up on the back porch at 3:15. The sound of their knocking sends Cal into a panic; he stands up and looks frantically around, as if for an alibi, and considers hiding in his room when he hears Mark's voice: "CAL!"

He goes to the back door. When he opens it, Mark shakes his head at him. "Are you really sick or what? Miss Crawford said nobody called you in."

Cal slapped his forehead. "I didn't think of that."

"You ditched?" Cory clamors in next to Mark. He has no backpack— he never does. Instead he has a clear plastic bag full of Warheads from Al's Smoke Shop behind the school.

"Kind of."

"She might call here tonight," Mark says. "I would unhook the phone."

Cory is quiet, looking around the kitchen. He holds out the bag to Cal. "Here, have some." He and Mark exchange glances as Cal rips open one of the Warheads. Cal pops it and screws his mouth up around the sourness. "Why are you looking at me like that," he says, squinting at them.

Cory asks, "How are you and your dad doing?" He sounds like his mother, who has left numerous messages on the machine at Cal's house, offering to make food for Brody and Cal.

"Fine." Cal looks away, reaches for the bag again. "You want to do something?"

"We saw your dad today," Mark says. He looks at Cory again.

Cal blinks. "You took a train?"

"No, at the library. Today was our field trip, remember? You missed it. We saw him there. He was sitting on the floor with books open everywhere. But just sitting there like he was sleeping." Mark shrugs, and there's something sly in his face that makes Cal stop sucking on the candy in his mouth.

"I guess he had a day off," Cory says, but he's not looking at Cal.

"He got fired," Mark says shortly. "My mom told me. Your dad got fired for being drunk on the train."

Cal feels the blood rushing to his forehead. "That's a lie, she doesn't even know him. And he leaves for work every day."

"Everyone knows about it."

Cory shuffles a little behind Mark, scratching at a mosquito bite on his arm. "Maybe he goes somewhere else. Maybe he always goes to the library."

"What for? You're lying. You came over just to tell me a stupid lie?"

"Sorry," Cory mumbles. He pushes the back door open and goes out. Mark lingers for a moment, and Cal thinks, *I never liked him anyway. I never did.* Mark says, "Just ask your dad and see what he says."

He goes out, and Cal slams the back door behind him and locks both locks. "Liar," he says. But he can't think of why Mark would lie, and he's startled at the idea that he and his father have both spent the day looking for things.

At three o'clock, Brody goes to Owl Lumber. The place is vaguely frightening to Brody, who grew up envious of the men who could walk into stores like these and be comfortable, even commanding, knowing exactly what they wanted and why. Men who, as boys, were building treehouses and shooting squirrels with BB rifles while Brody was reading books under his parents' kitchen table.

He smells sawdust, and then a complicated array of other scents that remind him of Christmas and then fruit and then baseball, one after another. He avoids eye contact with the two men behind the counter and moves quickly down the aisles, which are labeled with hanging signs: *Hickory. Poplar. Teak. Exotic Woods.* Past the main aisles is a section squared off from the rest, containing small shelves of oddly-colored wood in various shapes. Brody knows, somehow, without looking, but he searches for the hanging sign anyway: *Burl.*

It is strange to see the wood up close as opposed to in pictures. The store sells it in small chunks, in bowls, in thin rectangles advertised as molds for pens. There is oak burl and maple burl and walnut burl and other woods Brody has never heard of. He picks up a rhomboidal piece of maple burl, with its grain like tiny birds flying in a thousand directions. It has a smell that at first strikes him as unpleasant, but on his second breath, he realizes that it is simply more organic than the other wood. Eutrophic. Like old water, very still, loaded with uncontrolled growth. He breathes in again.

"Can I help you, sir?"

Brody nearly drops the burl. He turns and recognizes one of the men from the front of the store. "Uh, no, just looking around, thanks."

The man wears a plastic tag that reads "Jan" and his shirtsleeves are rolled up his elbows. He peers at Brody. "You got a project in mind? We have pen molds and good squares for bowls."

Brody wonders if he's being mocked. "I had an idea," he says, setting the maple burl back down on its shelf.

Jan waits, sucking on his lower lip.

"I was thinking about a boat," Brody says.

Jan blinks. "Building a boat? Out of what?"

"Burl."

"You want to use burl."

"Is that not possible?"

Jan blows air out from between pursed lips. "Uh, well, I've never heard of anybody trying it. You do realize how much wood that'd take? You know how much we charge just for a square foot of this stuff? Even the veneer is expensive." He pauses. "You done much carpentry?"

Brody shrugs. "Not a whole lot."

"You ever work with burl? You need to know it's almost impossible to work with. The grain goes all over the place. It resists everything you do to it, you know what I mean? It's impossible to know which way it's going to go."

Brody looks back at the shelf of burls. He picks up another one, much darker, with violet-black novas whorled across its surface.

"That's walnut burl," Jan says, more gently. "Best-looking one there is, if you ask me. But it's a matter of opinion. Pine's a good one too."

"So you don't think it can be done," Brody says.

"I didn't say that. I just said I've never heard of anybody trying it. But listen, if you're going to try it, you need to get a carpenter, if you don't mind me saying it. You could end up throwing a lot of good wood away if you don't do it right the first try. Carpentry's not like painting, you know? You can't start over. You get one cut and that's it."

"I didn't say I was a painter."

Jan lets out another puff of air. "Okay. Well, you know what I mean."

"Thanks for your help," Brody says. "I might be back."

Jan nods, already beginning to back away, and Brody wills himself to walk slowly out of the store. He knows he won't be back. He decides he'll have to find his own burl, or however many of them it will take, and do the cutting himself.

On the drive home, Brody promises himself that he will not watch the Lake Superior video again tonight, so as not to worry Cal. But he thinks of it, and then of the parts that are missing from it—the moments that now seem more precious because they weren't caught on that tape, weren't made undeniable.

Twilight had dropped softly like a light rain that last night they were there. Cal slept soundly in the backseat as Liz drove southwest, past Eagle Harbor and on toward Lac Labelle, a place she'd chosen on impulse off Brody's map. They were going to eat a late dinner out there, see what the water was like further down the peninsula.

They'd ended up stopping before Lac Labelle, though. Liz kept slowing the car at each small beach, scanning the sand as though for treasure, and the one that caught her eye and Brody's was Brunette Beach, where the diminishing light ignited a strange copper hue along the shoreline. Liz parked the car on a patch of gravel and twisted around to check on Cal. "He's out," she'd whispered, and she and Brody had climbed out of the car and locked it and walked slowly down the beach. When they reached the shoreline, they saw that it wasn't sand under the shallows, but wide, silky plates of scarlet stone dotted with perfect circles of white.

Brody had never seen anything like it and had to touch the stone under the water to be sure it was real. As Liz watched, her hair infused with rose from the sun, Brody knelt and found a slab that was smaller than the others, and his fingers worked around it, dislodging it. When he got a good grip on the edges, he hefted the stone up on one end and dragged it onto the dry sand. Still wet, the stone had the same satin sheen it had underwater, and Brody used his T-shirt to dry off its surface. The red and white became pale pink and cream in the weak sunlight. Liz reached down to trace the circles strewn across the stone's face, and Brody could smell metal in the rock.

"Look at that," Liz breathed, her face lifting, and Brody followed her gaze.

Before them, the water had turned the palest of blues. A narrow pathway of stones, pearly under the clouded light, led out into deeper water. The clouds were strung together in spirals and Brody had a sense of being inside something—a marble, a closed sphere. Then, as his eyes adjusted to the uninterrupted horizon, he realized that it was just the opposite: he was peering over some kind of edge, standing on the outskirts of what he knew. There was a foreignness in the purity of the place, in the waves' music; he thought of violins made of silver, but even that was too familiar to be right. He was deeply afraid, uncomprehending, but thrilled by it.

Liz said, "When the sun sets, those lights will be out again. The lanes for the ships to come in through. We should stay and wait to see them."

"All the way out here?"

She laughed. "Well, probably not. But I hope so. I want to see them."

Brody wanted to see them too—lights that arced out from the shoreline in glowing paths, meant to be a comfort, to guide boats in past the serrated teeth of stones. But he knew he wouldn't be able to understand the lines, how they could possibly do what they were supposed to do. The water seemed too wild to be tamed by light. It terrified him, that endless panorama, the idea of four hundred miles of waves. To Brody, it was an ocean, and they'd called it a lake.

In the morning, Cal listens for his father's movements. He can hear him dressing, but he knows he isn't going to work. The TV was on until after midnight last night—he could hear his mother's voice—and when he crept to the hallway to look, his father was in his same spot, though without the usual array of bottles across the table.

Normally his father is gone before Cal gets himself breakfast, but when he walks into the kitchen, his father is standing at the counter, making Cal's lunch.

"Aren't you going to work, Dad?" Cal asks, not looking at him.

"Not 'til later," his father says. He drops a Ziploc full of Doritos into a brown paper bag, followed by a container of sliced apples. "These okay? I know Mom gave you these."

"Yeah. When are you going?"

His father looks at him strangely, then goes to the fridge for peanut butter. "Oh, in an hour or so."

Cal wonders how he can ditch school if his father is staying in the house until after the bus comes. He considers hiding somewhere outside, but what if his father stays here for hours? There is Cory's treehouse, or the neighbor's toolshed, which is always unlocked. He glances out the window.

"Your bus will be here in a minute," his father says, giving him the same questioning look. "You all right? You're not feeling sick, are you?"

"I'm fine." Cal picks up his lunch off the counter, shoulders his backpack, and gives his father a brief hug. He goes out the front door, looks back at the living room windows, then curves quickly around the house into the neighbor's yard. He decides not to go into the toolshed, but to just sit down on the other side of it and wait for his father to leave.

It isn't a long wait. As soon as his father's car starts, Cal scrambles up from the grass and hurries to the back door, which he has a key to.

He sets his backpack and lunch down. He doesn't know what it is he wants to do with the day, but he knows he can't do it at school, around anyone else. Tapping his chin, he wanders down the hall and into his parents' bedroom.

There is a little pile of books and printed-out papers on the bedside table, and Cal sorts through these first. They are library books—*Woodworking, Woodworking for Beginners, Exotic Woods and their Histories.* The title of one of the printouts reads, "Conditions Conducive to Burl Growth." Cal has never seen any of this and he promises himself to look through it later. First things first. He looks around.

His parents have always had separate bookshelves. On the left are his father's books, thick and mostly paperback, and on the right, his mother's, which are all shapes and sizes and mostly hardcover. A tower of maps stands ready to fall next to some Britannicas, and Cal pulls the pile down and sits on the floor. He opens the first one—Canada. His fingers move over the wide blue spaces. He loves these—the big patches on maps, the ones with just a single word written across them, and nothing else, no cities or roads marked. The patches scare him a little but he thinks it's a good kind of scary. Cal stands up again, pulls down a couple of books. *Lost Discoveries* with a pharaoh's head and a golden discus on its shining cover. *Shifting Continents.* He's looked at this one with his mother, recognizes its pictures of the world before glaciers melted.

Cal gets up and crosses to the bureau. He knows that the bottom drawer is his mother's, and he wonders if his father has moved anything. He opens it and breathes in the scent of lemon. His mother has oddi-ties in here she used to let Cal touch when he asked—tiny leather bags filled with trinkets from her childhood, old notebooks with crumbly pages, Indian bead necklaces she'd gotten on a visit to a reservation when she was young. He wants to find something from the Lake Supe-rior trip—one of the rocks, maybe, that he remembers from a gift shop they'd gone into—but he doesn't see anything. He closes the drawer and his head drops against the bureau. The video, he thinks, might be the best thing they own.

Brody has inventoried his meager array of tools, kept on dusty plywood shelves in the basement, and has found a blunt axe and a saw that once belonged to his father-in-law. With the saw resting across the backseat, he drives south.

He begins his search with the woods that line the old prairie path, leaving the saw in the car and walking the length of Villa Park and Elmhurst before he gives up. He realizes it is a ridiculous plan to begin with, since there are houses just yards away from trail, and people would almost certainly hear him cutting and call the police.

He drives into LaGrange, a sprawling suburb dotted with Illinois forest preserves. He parks in the recreational lots and pushes past joggers and dog-walkers, taking the smaller, less-used trails into the thicker segments of the woods. The trees overwhelm him; it occurs to him that he hasn't been for a walk in the woods in years. He thinks of a Gustav Klimt painting he studied in college—was it *Birch Forest?* A simple pointillist painting, just slender trees bathed in fallen leaves, but the colors so carefully juxtaposed that if you stared hard enough, everything in the painting became one thing.

He studies the trunks of oaks, maples, walnuts, birch, looking for irregularities. He's fooled by an old bees' nest, then by a series of stumps from branches that had fallen or been cut away. The sudden bursts of movement from squirrels startle him, even irritate him; he feels that he won't be able to find a burl unless he is completely alone. He constantly looks behind him for fear that a park ranger will come by and figure out what he's doing.

After four hours, he gives up on the LaGrange preserves. He is exhausted but still exhilarated. Crossing the silver Cal Sag Channel on his way back toward Villa Park, he looks down at the water and sees a small barge, weighed down with stacks of wood. "Got burl?" he mutters, and almost laughs.

He decides to try the prairie path one more time, but further west, away from the suburbs. He leaves the car on a sidestreet in Glen Ellyn and cuts through the brush to the path, catching a spider web in his mouth as he goes. He fingers it off his teeth and starts walking with his head up, staring at the tree trunks.

He walks fifteen minutes before he stumbles upon a federally-owned preserve that is bordered by the path to the south and the westbound rail line to the north. The preserve is fenced off, but Brody finds a hole in the old wire and steps through. He can see the sun flashing across the tracks on the far side of the preserve. As he walks, he occasionally passes a tree with a massive nail lodged into its trunk, the words *PROPERTY OF THE MIDWESTERN RAILWAY* stamped into the iron. He tries to pull one out but it is immovable.

Most of the trees are dead, and the ground is extremely dry, which is a bad sign. *Burls can often be found in areas with high moisture problems or areas that have experienced sudden changes in conditions.* Brody looks for disease among the trees, but there is none. He wishes Liz were helping him do this. She would have found one by now; her eyes were always peeled for things. She'd loved endless hikes, was always trying to get Brody to take her to the Appalachians or back to the UP for them, though Brody never wanted to go. He was always renovating something in the house, or reworking the garden, or something that made those trips seem untimely. It annoyed him, her always wanting to leave.

Liz, he had always thought, was in love with opacity. He'd told her that when they were still dating, and she'd laughed, misunderstanding him. It wasn't that she was indirect, or contradictory. It was that she loved to be mystified. She'd buy 2,000 piece puzzles and be disappointed when they were finished. She loved the huge, monochromatic spaces on maps. She was like that even in the last hour Brody spent with her.

There were just Brody and the nurse in the room when Liz died. The cancer had spread so quickly that there was nothing to be done but wait, and that was what Brody did, wait, almost unmoving, though he kept sending Cal off to school every day because he didn't want him to see this, his mother fading into the background of the pale-walled room they'd given her. She was heavily medicated against pain, but she was alert, waiting for Cal's brief visits after school, listening as Brody read to her in the late evenings when a neighbor stayed with Cal.

On the night it happened, the nurse, who wore a cross around her neck, was sitting on one side of the bed and Brody was on the other. Liz was sleeping lightly while Brody read in low tones out of a Stephen Hawking book. The nurse, Cassie, looked at Brody and whispered, "Why do you read her that?"

"She likes this kind of stuff," he mouthed. He tried to smile.

"It's too hard to understand," the nurse responded, barely whispering. She tried a grin, too, leaning forward a little. "It made my head spin."

Brody looked at Liz, still asleep. He turned a few pages, stopping at a vibrant photograph of a supernova. He showed Cassie. "You know what this is?"

"Baby stars," Liz murmured.

Brody dropped the book against her legs. "Sorry," he said, picking it back up. He looked at Liz, whose eyes blinked and then closed again. "Sorry, honey. What did you say?"

"A star nursery. That's what they make when they explode." Her voice was surprisingly strong, even coming out muffled by the pillow. "It's not as sad as they make out."

Cassie laughed. "I love her," she said to Brody. Then, to Liz, "Did you take physics in college, Mrs. O'Connell?"

Burl Wood

Liz's hair, still thick and dark since they hadn't even tried chemo, was splayed out across the pillow. Brody reached out and gently combed through it with his fingers. He waited for her to respond, but she didn't.

Cassie, from the way Brody remembered it, seemed to know right away. She closed her eyes, prayed something inaudibly, and stood up. But Brody didn't understand it; he swore he could still see the blanket moving gently above Liz's shoulders. Then he thought he saw something else—another movement, first of that blanket, and then of the white curtains behind the bed. He tried to follow the movement but it eluded him, as though it found a clear path to the door and slipped out without colliding with any other material thing. He looked at the door, then back to Liz, and it was like coming down off a staircase where there is one less step than you expect there to be. He dropped.

There is a woodpecker somewhere overhead; the tapping seems to snap the air above Brody in two. Brody passes his hands over his face, hard. He trains his eyes against the sun until he sees it, and then the bird disappears into a hollow and the woods fall silent again. "Don't try pecking through a burl, friend," Brody mutters. "You'll embarrass yourself." His gaze shifts left, and he sees it.

At first, it seems impossible that a burl could be so enormous. Swelling from the torso of a thick maple, the burl is deeply ribbed like coral, ovular in shape and the color of old ivory. It is the length of Brody's arms outstretched.

"Hey, there," Brody says. "Hey, okay." He circles the tree; the burl is so big he can see it from the other side of the trunk. He comes back around and eases his palm over the burl's broad curve. With his hand still on the burl, he looks up into the tree's branches. No leaves; the bark is grey and peeling. He believes the tree to be dead, which means that the burl may or may not be rotted inside.

"It's worth it," he says, and steps back to measure the burl's size. It might take two, three hours to saw it down. And he will have to do it after nightfall, as quietly as possible.

He looks north, to where the sun's last rays glint off the railroad tracks, and wonders how loud the cutting will be.

Cal sits in the kitchen, his science textbook open in front of him, with some papers scattered across the tabletop to give the illusion of having been at school all day. He has eaten the lunch his father prepared and carefully stashed the trash away in his closet.

When Brody walks in, mumbling to himself, Cal straightens up and starts reading.

"Hey, pal," his father says from the kitchen doorway. "How was school? Got a lot of homework?"

"Not too bad," Cal says, avoiding his father's eyes.

"I'm starved. You want pizza?" Brody opens the freezer, shuffles some boxes around. "We're down to pizza and fish sticks, and we know how you feel about those."

"Pizza."

"Okay."

Cal balances his book on its spine and peers over the edge at his father as he unwraps the frozen pizza and hunts around for a pan. "Next to the oven," Cal says softly.

"Oh. Right." His father fishes out the pizza pan and turns the oven on. His back still to Cal, he says, "So, how much homework do you have, exactly?"

Cal ponders. "Well, not a whole lot."

"Can you take some time off from it tonight? Help me out with something? It'll be an adventure."

Cal sets the book down. His father, turning back to him from the oven, sticks his hands into his jeans pockets and stands there waiting.

"What kind of adventure?"

"I want to cut down a burl off a tree. I want to use the wood for something. You know what a burl is?"

"It's when a tree gets cancer." Cal says it and then clamps his teeth together, horrified.

"How did you know that?" His father's mouth is agape.

"I saw your—your stuff. I read some of it."

"When?"

Now they stare at each other, and Cal looks away first. "I ditched school. Two days in a row."

His father considers. "I got fired."

"I know."

"You know?"

"My friends at school—" Cal stops.

"Oh, kid. I'm really not doing well here, huh? I haven't been much of an example. I'm sorry, Cal, I really am." He sits down heavily at the table, staring blankly at Cal's book. "I'm sorry."

"It's okay."

"No, it isn't. Cal, promise me you won't be skipping any more school. You know what, forget the bus—I'll drive you until I find another job. I'm sorry if you've been getting a hard time at school because of me."

They sit in silence for awhile and then Brody gets up to retrieve the pizza. "You know this kind of thing is bad for us both," he murmurs from the stove as he cuts the crust with sewing scissors. Cal remains silent, not sure what his father is talking about.

"I should learn to cook."

"*That* sounds like it could be bad for us," Cal says. His father laughs, and Cal lets out a breath.

"You're probably right, but even so. Now, about tonight. Will you help?" Brody sets two slices of the pizza next to Cal's book.

"Okay."

"Good man. We're out of here as soon as it's dark. We're going out-side. You need dark clothes and sneakers."

Cal doesn't ask questions. As he eats he watches his father's move-ments in the kitchen, the way he briefly touches Cal's mother's things, as though looking for what's different.

At eight o'clock they park the car next to a Glen Ellyn playground that backs up into the prairie path. Brody and Cal walk west in the darkness, Brody holding a flashlight and Cal tightly bundled in a winter coat. In his other arm, Brody carries his father-in-law's saw in its leather case. When they reach the preserve, Brody moves slowly along the fence until he finds the hole in the wire and then he helps Cal through. "Okay, this is it," he says softly. "It should be a little ways north of here. Stay close to me."

He finds it within minutes, letting out a little whoop that surprises Cal. "Still there," he says, holding the beam of his flashlight on the swell of wood.

"*That?*"

"I know."

"Dad, it's huge."

"I know."

Cal's father kneels in the dirt, sliding the saw out of its leather case. "Okay," he says softly. "Now we wait. You can sit down, Cal. Stay warm. Stay out of sight. Hold onto the flashlight for me."

"Do you really think people are watching us?"

His father laughs quietly. "No, I doubt it. But just in case. You clear on what we're doing?"

Cal nods. "As soon as we hear a train, you get up and start cutting, and I keep watch. When the train's gone, we hide again. We do it until you've got the burl down."

"You got it."

Cal sits, feeling the nub of a tree root underneath him. He rubs his hands together inside the coat, and he watches the railroad tracks. The tracks, drawing a line between the preserve and the outskirts of the suburbs, are dark and glimmering in the faint light of streetlamps from the other side. There is no moon. Cal thinks he can hear a phone ringing somewhere on the other side of the tracks. Then a dog barking. He realizes his heart is pounding.

"Any minute now," his father whispers. He doesn't wear a watch; he doesn't need to, not when it comes to trains. He's crouched below the burl, eyeing it, as if deciding where to cut before he touches it. The burl looks much larger to Cal in the darkness, but not ominous; he thinks of a boat, turned on its side and balanced vertically against a wall. He thinks of the video.

"We'll make a canoe out of it," his father says hoarsely.

Cal squints at his father, startled. "What did you say?"

His father says, "A boat."

"Dad . . . I don't know if that could work. I read about it. I mean—I want a boat too but you could never do that."

His father's expression is unreadable in the darkness. "Well, Cal, it can't hurt us to try, can it? We'll make something out of it."

Then Cal hears it: the grating of wheels on iron, the first whistle. He thinks, *a steamer*. The ground trembles beneath him and he rises into a crouch. When the train barrels around the bend and starts down the long straightaway through the woods, Cal leaps up. "Now, Dad," he almost yells.

But his father is already up and cutting, his arms moving fast but with a steadiness that amazes Cal. As the train roars past, the sound of the sawing is lost momentarily in the clamor, but Cal readjusts and then through the shriek of wheels he can hear his father's saw: *sea-bound, sea-bound.* His father's rhythm suddenly overrides the train's. Cal comes close, just close enough to see the glint of the blade without crowding his father. In the intermittent light that sparkles between the train cars, Cal can see the layer of sweat, like rain on a window, glistening on his father's neck. Then the last car passes, and his father drops the saw and goes down on his knees.

"Jesus Christ," he wheezes.

"You okay?" Cal drops with him, leaning forward to look at his father.

"Oh, yeah. I am. It's hard work when you've got to do so much—" he breathes, "so fast." He wipes the sweat away from his eyes, reaches back to pull at his shoulder muscles. "Jesus."

"How many more?"

"Cuts?"

"Trains."

"Four freights for sure, if there are no signal delays. And three passenger. I'll need at least that."

"What if no more come?"

"Oh, they'll come. I know that much."

They wait.

Seven trains pass. And when it's over, the ground lurches under Cal's feet with the impact of the burl. Leaves fly and scatter in all directions. Brody falls to his knees again, then flat on his back, heaving. Cal picks up the flashlight. He trains the beam on the prize that lies on the forest floor between them. He waits for his father to stagger over to his side and look down.

Together they stare at the burl. They won't know until they open it. Its time might have passed; its insides might be rank and rotted, beyond salvage. But they also might have caught it at just the right moment, when opening its hard-won center would reveal the wildest of grains, nebulous and unknowable, beautiful beyond compare in its capacity for weathering all things.

On the French Coast

There are no guests at the Harbor Lights Motel this time of year, when Lake Superior has turned frigid and the winds coming off the water are cold enough to split the cuticles on your fingertips. But sometimes Parker and I will get a straggler or two asking for a single night, and just in case, I've made a last trip out for groceries, and when I come back, Parker is shoveling the front walkway. His hood is pulled low so that all I can see is the glow of his cigarette, but when I come up the walk he pushes the hood back. He says, "Can we go inside for a second?"

"If you help me put the groceries away."

Parker leaves the shovel next to the entryway and opens the door for me. I go in with the bags and line them up on the kitchen counter. I feel a headache coming on and I sit down at the table and stretch my arms out in front me. "I don't know if I can take another winter," I say.

Parker hovers in the doorway, not touching the groceries. He clears his throat. "Gordie called."

I stare at him. "You're kidding."

He doesn't meet my eyes. "He's coming back to Marquette for a few weeks. He's been in Baltimore, apparently. He wanted to know if we all felt like getting together. The five of us. He asked where Abe and Macy were."

"He asked—"

"He doesn't know. I didn't tell him, either. How would I do that?"

37

"How could he not know?" I say. "How is that even possible?" But we both know how, and the question just hangs there. Parker leans against the wall with his hands in his pockets, and the snow melting off his boots leaves pools of water on the linoleum. He looks down, heels the boots off, and then sits down heavily across from me.

We don't speak. I turn in my chair and look out the window at the Lake. It's a white desert this time of year, and the sun is weak on its surface. I hear Parker sigh. I close my eyes.

I can see it perfectly, if only because I have forced myself to look back on it over and over again, as a kind of penance: the five of us standing on a cliff in Normandy, staring down into the sea. We are from a coastline of our own, the bright cold boardwalks of Marquette, Michigan, and we have come here thinking we'll find an echo of home, something to calm us. Paris has been too frenetic for us—the thickly-scented streets, the tented peddlers, the churches that stab into the sky and offer a view of the city that looks to us like a continent of piled jigsaw pieces.

On our way here, we occupy two sets of seats on a second-class train going from Gare St. Lazare to Cherbourg. Parker and I sit together and across from us are my twin brother Abe and our friends Macy and Gordie. We've just graduated from college. Parker, hand in mine, has his eye on the green fields racing past us, like he's mentally planting seeds. He's planning to run his cousin's vineyard near Petoskey when we get back. Macy's small bag is bulging with fruit she bought from a cart outside our hostel. She's tighter with her money than the rest of us and won't eat at the cafes; she'll be starting an internship in New York in autumn and has been saving up for two years.

Next to her, Gordie in a pinstriped shirt cleans his sunglasses and grins at his tiny reflection in the lenses. Gordie is our scientist; he has a Stephen Hawking book with him on the train and loves to explain things like the refraction of light. When Abe tries to slap the glasses out of Gordie's hand, Gordie says, "Comb your hair. You look like the swamp thing." Abe rolls his eyes and sits back. He thinks he might work for Parker's cousin, but has also applied to the maritime academy in Traverse City. I have no plan other than Parker, and all I want right now is to get back to Michigan, where our future is plotted to the day.

When the train pulls into Cherbourg, Abe gives himself a little shake and leans forward to peer out the window. "This is *it?*"

We look. There is a tiny bus station on a yellow street, and far, far behind that we can see the dark rise of trees.

"This is it," Parker says. "Cherbourg. Let's go."

We go into the station, where an elderly woman behind a desk tells us there are several buses running throughout the afternoon, going back and forth from Cherbourg to the American Cemetery and Omaha Beach. Abe, who has been reading war history textbooks since he was ten, pipes up, "We want the next bus. We want both places. Five tickets." She wrinkles her nose a little at him—he's wearing a tee shirt with a silver skull pictured on it—but hands him the tickets.

We're the only ones on the bus, and we spread out, enjoying the space. Macy, with her purple-rimmed glasses and tight black curls, is the low-maintenance one; she folds in on herself with her knapsack on her lap as she watches the town pass by. The rest of us carry bulky backpacks loaded with Aquafina bottles and Heath Bars, a couple of big flasks in Abe's case, and we leave them all over the bus.

Gordie sits on the aisle across from Macy, his dark gaze on the mirror above the bus driver's head. Abe is right behind the driver, asking questions; in the middle of it all, Parker's hand makes a small bowl over mine and when I look at him, the afternoon sun ignites the hazel in his eyes. He murmurs, "This will be like going home for a little while, Leah. You'll see. Once we see the water." As he says this, we pass a bright placard on the roadside that reads, *Welcome Americans.*

The driver takes us to the Cemetery first. He pulls into a small lot hemmed in with trees and turns around to face us as we gather up our bags. "I've got a card for you to take with you," he says. His English is perfect. "This is only bus that comes, so don't forget to be back here for one of those times."

Abe is fussing with his bag, and so I push down the aisle first. The driver hands me a small card with a list of the return times hand-written on it. "Thanks," I say. He smiles at me. Tufts of graying hair peek out from under his cap. "Are you here for someone from your family?" he asks.

It takes me a second to understand his question. "Oh, no," I say. I look at the time card. "No."

"Well," the driver says. "I'm sure it will mean a lot to you, even so. It's a special place."

I nod and start down the bus steps. The air outside is cool and fresh, and I breathe deeply. Abe, awkwardly shouldering his bag, comes out after me and stumbles on the steps, cursing as he lands on his knees. "Brilliant," he says. He shakes his long, tangled hair out of his eyes as he reaches for my outstretched hand.

"Break anything?" Parker asks, coming down the steps behind him with Macy and Gordie in tow.

"You mean something in my body or something in my bag?"

I roll my eyes. "Come on already."

We follow a pale red walkway to the Cemetery, moving under a thick overhang of trees. We can hear the faint murmur of a crowd, but we are alone on the path. When we emerge into the open we all stop, blinking in the sudden blast of sun. The cemeteries we have known at home are the size of a small parking lot, fenced in and strewn with red and grey stones. Here we face an enormous reflecting pool bearing bright green lilies, flanked by two American flags fluttering from poles like skyscrapers, and two fields of innumerable white crosses on either side of a stone chapel, structured like a gazebo, in the distance. All of it backs up into a dark forest, and beyond the northern perimeter is the coast; we can taste sea salt and feel the breeze rising up from our right.

"Damn," Parker says. He runs both hands through his hair. "Guess we made a good call."

"This is incredible," Gordie murmurs. "Hold on one second, guys. I want to get this view." He pulls his camera out and begins toying with the focus. I step out of his way. He is careful, aiming the lens at the northern border and exhaling slowly just before he snaps the photo.

When he's finished, we continue down the walkway. The sun simmers in my hair, but I don't feel stifled as I did in the city. The water in the reflecting pool is startlingly blue, and I wonder if there is purpose in the colors: red walkway, white gravemarkers, blue water. Behind me, Abe sounds like a newscaster: "Seventy acres. Over nine thousand dead."

"How should we go?" Gordie asks from behind his camera. "Should we walk around the perimeter or go through?"

I realize he means through the crosses, and from this distance, it seems an impossible thing to do; they almost form a wall, blending together on the green. But Macy says, "I want to go through the middle. I'd like to see them up close."

We walk slowly, following one of several paths that cut through the green. Up close, the markers are made of pearly stone that glitters in the sun. Some of the crosses have names; many don't. The nameless ones read, "Here lies in honored glory a comrade in arms, known but to God." The last four words startle me. I picture a soldier lying in the sand, his face turned down, and wispy white arms reaching down for him. I step away from the stone and take Parker's arm.

Gordie says, "I wonder how many have no names."

I point at Abe. "Ask the encyclopedia."

"I don't know everything," he says.

Parker walks in a small circle with me, pointing out the last names that sound familiar to us. "Midwesterners," he says. "Michiganders."

"Not necessarily," I say. "'Adams'? He could be from anywhere."

Macy crouches down in front of a marker that has a Star of David at its apex instead of a cross. "This one was a Jewish soldier," she says without turning around.

"Well, obviously," I say.

"I'm just saying, this is the first one I've seen so far."

"They have your religion stamped on your dog tags," Abe informs us. "So if you get torn up beyond recognition they can still give you the kind of burial you want."

Macy stands up, cringing. I say, "That's lovely, Abe."

"Move out of the way a little, guys," Gordie says, bringing up his camera. He backs up a few steps and photographs the far treeline, lifting the camera a little higher with each shot. It's a perfect angle; the trees in the distance are green-black, making hard waves against the bluest sky we've seen in days.

"Get the water," I say. Gordie obligingly turns north, and Macy moves up behind him. "Don't you think this is a little weird?" she mutters.

"Weird?" Gordie says tonelessly, focused on the camera.

"Weird. You're taking pictures of the trees. Like this is a nature walk or something."

I look over at Macy. Her skinny arms are crossed in front of her chest like she's cold, and she is chewing her lower lip. "He's just getting the scenery," I say. "Jesus."

Gordie lowers the camera and turns back to Macy. "You want me to get the Star of David?"

"Okay."

He follows her back to the marker and kneels down a few feet in front of it, eyes narrowed. He takes a couple of shots. "Okay, Macy, I've got it for you," he says. "It looks pretty amazing with all the crosses at an angle behind it. Come here and look, though. I could do it differently if you want."

Macy goes to his side and peers through the lens. "It looks like a comet with the tails behind it," she says.

As the two of them bend together over the camera, Parker turns in a circle, hand shading his eyes. "God, it's so green," he murmurs. "Did you see how green it was, on the way here? All the little rivers? The things you could grow out here."

"Grow? Get your mind out of the grape sties," Abe says. "We're in Europe, for fuck's sake." He mops some sweat off his brow with the hem of his tee shirt. He'd slept for most of the train ride, Gordie pulling lint off him as he sat slumped against the window.

"'Sties'?" Parker narrows his eyes at him. "Isn't that where you want to work this summer?"

Abe shrugs. He's looking past us. "I didn't say I wanted to do anything for sure. What the hell is Gordie doing? Are we initialing the sidewalk now?"

We look; Gordie is crouched on the red walkway, scraping at it with a shard of rock. We move up behind him and lean over his shoulder. I let out a moan. "'Freedom Isn't Free'? Are you serious, Gordie? Come on."

Gordie turns around and shrugs. "I don't know. It seems like a good thing to write. I want to write something here before we go. Leave a mark." He bends back over the walkway, going over the letters a second time. I remember him doing something like this at Homecoming last fall—etching all of our names into the wooden slats of the deck where we were photographed.

"You could at least pick a line out of poem," Abe says. "Make it a little deeper than that. Or a quote from Stephen Ambrose or something."

"Okay," Macy says. "Or how about you just let him write what he wants? It means something to him."

"Of course you'd say that," Abe says. "Poet fucking laureate of Michigan. You'd probably write things on the headstones if they let you."

Parker clears his throat. He shoves his tanned, muscled hands into his pockets and looks uncomfortably at me. I know that he's as baffled by Macy as I am—Macy, who has spent the last four years working on a marketing degree, but who probably has some folded-up Auden in her knapsack right now, and who does bizarre things like write verse in the condensation on mirrors. Just this morning, I found a line, blurred beyond legibility, in the mirror in the hostel bathroom. I couldn't see my reflection through it and so I wiped it away.

"Anyway," Abe says, "I need a drink."

"Oh for Pete's sake," Parker says. "Right now? It's four o'clock in the afternoon."

"No one said you had to be involved." Abe goes off, and because Gordie and Macy are back to experimenting with the camera, I lean into Parker.

"What's he going to do? Drink in the restroom?" Parker mutters. "Seriously, Leah, he needs to slow it down. I get it that he's celebrating, but he needs to take it easy."

I watch Abe move down the walkway toward the visitors' center. I'm just happy he graduated; it was close. He was the only one of the five of us who didn't have gold or silver ropes to go over his robe, and when our parents started taking pictures, he said he had to meet some friends and disappeared into the crowd outside the gymnasium.

I want to follow him now, as I did then, but I doubt that he needs my reassurance. That's because I don't know that he's already been rejected from the maritime academy, or that he'll lie to me about the next four jobs he gets fired from. I don't know how bad things will be in St. Ignace, where he ends up working a dock by day and drinking alone at night; he'll be too convincing on the phone. "I'll be running the show in a couple of months," he'll say. "I told you Petoskey was a dead-end idea." I won't know anything about my brother, really, until I find him in a squalid apartment, sleeping on packing boxes next to a heap of bottles and a sandwich green as algae. Right now, I'm satisfied with thinking that Abe is just a little unruly, like a lot of people we went to school with.

When Gordie approaches us, he is hugging himself, the camera dangling from a rubber clasp around his arm. He leans in close to Parker and me. "So is there someone Jewish in Macy's family?" he asks softly. "Something we didn't know?"

Parker's forehead crinkles. "What?"

"She's putting flowers down by the Star of David. She's really got a thing about it."

I follow his gaze to Macy, who is kneeling in front of the marker, arranging some yellow blooms that I recognize from the shrubs around the perimeter. She forms a semicircle with the blooms, seems to consider, then gets up and walks quickly toward the bushes. She looks around before tearing off a few more. I laugh.

"What's funny?" Gordie squints at me through the sun.

"Nothing," I say. I touch his arm. "Nothing. I just like that she stole the flowers off the bushes. It's definitely something she'd do." I have the quick, nervous twinge I often have with Gordie, when I've said something that inexplicably hurts him. I look to Parker for help, but he's adrift, scanning the opposite end of the cemetery, probably for Abe.

"Well, don't say that to her," Gordie says.

"I won't."

Macy wanders back to us, and the four of us walk on toward the stone chapel, where a crowd of tourists mills about, waiting to get in. Out of the corner of my eye I see a small face bobbing up and down among the crosses, and I blink. It's a little boy in red coveralls, wandering between the crosses, craning his neck. I think I hear him say, "Grandma," but I'm not sure.

"Hey guys," I say. "Look at that little kid over there. He's alone. What the heck."

"I don't see his parents around," Macy says. "Should we go over there? He's probably lost."

"I'll go," I say, but Gordie cuts in front of me, working his way down the rows to where the child, hand in his mouth, is now standing still. As Gordie bends low, I imagine him with his own child, and glance over at Macy. She's watching Gordie, too, but a nameless something in her eyes tells me this is not a woman in love.

I can just barely hear what Gordie says to the child: "Your grandma? What color shirt is she wearing?"

The boy says, "White."

When I'm thinking that there are fifty women on the premises wearing white tee shirts, Gordie asks, "What does she have in her hands?"

I don't hear the boy's answer, but Gordie takes the child's hand and then the two of them walk further away from us. The boy's arm comes up; he points to a small group hovering near the treeline. In a moment Gordie leads him over to an elderly woman carrying a big green tote bag. He converses with her in a low murmur and the woman laughs, bringing her hand up to her mouth.

Parker sighs. "He's a pro," he says. "He makes it look so easy."

I nod, watching him. Gordie, I think, is the kind of person who will make life in general look easy. He'll marry a girl who adores him and they'll have four kids. He'll get the lab technician job he's been studying for, and he'll love it, because he will work hard, but there will always be time for his family.

So it will be a shock to me, and to Parker, when we learn that Gordie has been beaten half to death outside a bar in Terre Haute. By then, we'll at least know why; he'll have come out to us. I'll remember a conversation from the week he left for his graduate program: "I can't go to school any closer to home than this," he'd said. "Honestly, my father's going to slit my throat one of these days." It won't be his dad, it'll be two guys he's never seen before, but somehow this will seem worse. Gordie will have nowhere to go. He won't come to us, no matter how many times we call his apartment. He'll change his answering machine to an automated recording, as though just letting people hear his voice will leave him too unguarded.

"Here he comes," Macy says. She pulls her hair back and I can see dark green stains on her fingertips. "And there's Abe, too. He doesn't look too good, Leah."

"I noticed."

Macy shakes her head. "Maybe we should head right back after this so he can get some more sleep." She says it like she's stating the obvious, and I swear that she's accusing me of something.

"He won't have it," I say shortly. "I promise. But you're welcome to run that by him yourself."

Abe and Gordie fall into step together on their way back to us, and Abe, next to Gordie with his flushed skin and dark eyes, really does look ghostly. He nods briefly at us. "Have you hit the chapel yet?" he demands. "I want to go in there."

"No," Parker says. "You go ahead of us."

I look at him; he's unreadable. Macy and Gordie follow Abe down the walkway toward the chapel and in a minute they are hovering at the entrance, waiting for the space to clear. Macy digs into her knapsack and then hands Abe a bright yellow apple. He takes it.

"Well?" I say, turning back to Parker.

Parker shakes his head. "Come over here. We can go in there in a second if you want to."

His arm around my shoulders, he leads me off the main path toward the trees. "It's beautiful here, isn't it?" he asks softly.

I reach up and push some of his sandy hair back from his forehead. "It is," I say. "And coming here was Abe's idea, remember? We owe him one. We could still be in Paris."

"Listen," he says. He pulls me down to the grass and we sit side-by-side, facing the crosses that become, at this level, like a forest of tiny birch trees. "When we get home, I'm going to take that job with my cousin. You know that. But first, I want to go somewhere, just the two of us. Maybe back to the Porcupine Mountains. No jobs, no distractions, no worrying about anything. Like we used to talk about."

I say, "I know." It's the thing I've been waiting for him to bring up. In my own way, I've been planning this trip, and the proposal that I'm sure will come with it, for months.

With Parker's arm around me, I completely forget about the cemetery; instead I have an odd flashback, remembering how we played together as children and how one Sunday after church we decided to remake the Garden of Eden in Parker's den. We brought in bag after bag of leaves and dumped them on the floor. We ripped up gardens in the neighborhood and brought in the flowers. It was innocent, but when his parents saw what we had done, they told us to go and apologize to everyone we'd stolen flowers from. Instead Parker and I went around with Scotch tape and tried to put the flowers back where we'd gotten them.

I laugh, and Parker looks at me with that smile I love, the one that accentuates the tiny white scar on his upper lip. "So you want to?" he asks.

I do. Tonight in our hostel room, when I'm thinking nothing about this place, I'll put my bracelet with its iridescent blue beads under his pillow—a code language we've devised for *I love you*. A month from now, I'll go on this getaway he has planned. He'll take me up to the Keweenaw Peninsula, and on Brockway Mountain, with Lake Superior spread out below us like a blue satin shirt buttoned with clouds, he'll propose.

I won't know how I'll feel four years into our marriage, when we've tried everything and can't conceive, and when Parker, driving me home from the hospital after our final attempt at in vitro, sits out the green light on Cedar until the cars are piled behind us with their horns blaring. I won't know that when Abe comes apart a year after that, I'll choose him over Parker, saying, "I'm stretched too thin. I can't." I can't even imagine the way Parker's vineyard will look the last time I see it: ochre skeletons bowed in the wind.

Right now, what I know is the glow of grapevines in season. Parker has been taking me out there since we were teenagers. We had our first kiss there; his taste was migrant and alive, like apples and wicker, and we were canopied in purplish reds and greens. When my brother and our two friends come back to us from across the lawn, it is as though I cast those colors back onto them, because they look suddenly untouch-able. Even Abe's step has quickened. I see strong limbs and bright eyes that soak in light and color as readily as a child's.

"This guy in the chapel said there's an overlook on the edge of the cemetery," Abe says, pointing. "He said we'd get a full view of the water. We should check it out if you two are done with your secret conference."

"Perfect," Parker says. We get up together and Gordie takes out his camera again, murmuring about a panoramic lens. Parker's hand lingers for a second in my back pocket, and later, I'll find a crushed blossom there.

We drift away from the chapel, down another stone pathway toward the water. The overlook is set a good ways apart from the cemetery, and it is only when we step onto it that we realize how high up we actually are. A cobblestone ledge is the only barrier between us and the waves far below. The horizon is uninterrupted.

We stand in a line, hands on the brick ledge. We peer out at the water. Midnight blue depths in the distance slowly give way to peridot shallows. The cliffs to the left and right are like massive green waves held in place. A cottony mist shrouds the furthest of the cliffs, and there is no way of telling what lands lie beyond them, whether they are connected to the ground we stand on. Parker pulls me up against him.

Abe, eyes on the water, says, "It doesn't seem possible that so many people died out here."

I can feel Parker nodding. "It doesn't," he says softly. His body shifts a little. "You know, I haven't even been thinking about it. You're right. It doesn't seem possible."

"I can't imagine it." It is Macy's voice, barely audible; she's a little apart from us, leaning way over the ledge and clutching the stone to hold herself steady. "I just—can you imagine how it was for the soldiers who saw all this from the other side? I mean when they were rushing the shore from the boats, knowing that they were going to die. I don't understand how they did it."

When nobody says anything, Macy goes on: "I think maybe the ones that died here were dead before they got to shore. I think they made some kind of change before the bullets hit them. They left themselves. They had the chance to make that decision. You know? They were somewhere else when their bodies ran up the beach."

Parker is frozen behind me. I stare at Macy, but she doesn't look at me. Abe says, "I think I get you," at the same time Gordie says, "*God,* Macy."

There is another, longer silence. At last I say, "Way to ruin the moment, guys."

Abe laughs; he's a little drunk, of course, but still, I'm grateful for it. Macy blushes. "You're right," she says, shaking her head. "That was kind of morbid. Sorry."

Abe says, "You know what? It's just damn beautiful. That's what matters." He throws out his arm. "*Look* at this."

As if in response, Gordie's camera goes off, and the bright chirp of it breaks the spell. Parker brings up our next stop—the Netherlands—and we start arguing about what we'll do there. Abe wants to get obliterated. Parker wants to go into the countryside on bicycles. We talk on. We watch the water, the silver-capped waves.

Still, it is a relief when a crowd of other tourists squeezes onto the overlook, snapping photos and pulling children back from the ledge. To my right, a Coke hisses open. A woman asks me to take a picture of herself and her husband with their backs to the water. Then someone asks Parker for the time, and we realize we're about to miss our bus.

We'll take that bus to Omaha Beach, where the sand will gleam red under the falling sun. There will be people in bathing suits. When Parker wonders aloud if people ought to be swimming in that water,

Abe will say, "Think about it. If our soldiers hadn't fought here, this wouldn't be a place where you *could* swim. Of course you should swim here." We'll wander down the beach to an isolated spot and wade in together in our shorts and tees.

When our trip has ended, we'll fly out of Germany. Going through customs, I'll fight with a security guard, begging him to let me take home my Aquafina bottle loaded with sand and shells from Omaha Beach. He'll be adamant at first, but when I conjure up a story about my grandfather dying there, he'll relent, waving me on. I'll carry my souvenir onto the plane like a trophy. We'll go home, where things will start to go wrong.

Eventually, I'll move in with Abe and stay with him until he's well again and able to find another job. Parker will come back to me after a two-year separation and say he's willing to try again. Gordie will disappear into another city and will fade into a background where we hope he is happy. But Macy, Macy in the midst of it all, will be in the second of the two towers on September 11th, and she will have to choose between leaping from a window and burning alive. She'll jump. She'll make the shift, the way the soldiers did, rushing the cliffs from the ocean: when she takes that breath, she will already be gone, out of this world. Her body will fall, its shape eclipsing from view the true ascent of her.

This is a thing I think about often, but never for too long. Because I cannot think of a way to atone for that moment, or for that day, when the five of us were together on the French coast.

We were twenty-one. We saw the sea and it was beautiful, jade and blue; we smelled salt in the air. A thousand white crosses at our backs couldn't quite make us believe in death.

Transmissions

Lately I keep coming back to the fact that I was better at life in the seventh grade. It's true that back then I spent most of my time trying to dig up fossils in the backyard, or pasting glow-in-the-dark trilobites to my walls while my friends were experimenting with mascara and eye shadow, but I'm pretty sure I had some kind of grip on life. Everyone—the ice cream truck driver, the mailman, the cashiers at the Dominick's—knew that I intended to be a paleontologist who would eventually discover a new and, best case scenario, extraterrestrial life form. At seven I was convinced that I had already come close to it in the form of white noise, which I believed to be comprised of alien transmissions. The obsession never really went away.

I have wondered if maybe my passion for aliens was what ultimately led to my being paid to clean up bleachers, having a tattooed daughter who breaks into water parks at night and an ex-husband with the nickname Pug.

But I know that wasn't it. I think my problem in high school and college was that I was too emotional about everything, had an overwhelming sense of the romantic. I mean I remember that I cried when I saw a slide of a supernova in my freshman year physics class at U of I. When Professor Roth asked me what was wrong, I said something like, "It's just so beautiful" and had to get up and leave. I was a prime candidate for falling in love, doing something stupid, and ruining my life.

I'm rolling up to the Portillo's drive-thru in my Jeep when my phone starts singing. It's really singing, or more like screaming—some punk song my daughter programmed into my phone for me. It's her, Christina, and as usual she talks over my hello: "Hey Fran, where's my black pullover, did you wash it or something?" She is seventeen and has just started this first-name business.

"Welcome to Portillo's, can I take your order?"

"Hold on, hon," I say into the phone. "Give me a piece of chocolate cake. Actually no, a chocolate cake shake. A large. The biggest one."

"That's disgusting, Fran, and so unhealthy," Christina says.

"I have every right to chocolate. I don't bark at you for smoking cigarettes, do I?"

"Bite me. Where's my sweater?"

"It's probably in the dryer."

Christina hangs up. I get my cake shake.

I don't know what she wants with a black sweater. It's a Chicago July, hot as hell, and I've been lugging my floor fan around the house with me like an I.V. I hope she's not planning on sneaking into some place after dark. It was two weeks ago that she and her boyfriend put on army camo and sneaked into the abandoned water park down Route 83. They didn't get caught, but Jace dropped a lightpost onto Christina's foot and she had to be taken to a doctor. I never got the story on how a lightpost was picked up and dropped. But it happened.

I've been picking up the remains of taffy apples and hot pretzels for the last seven hours, and every time I do this I swear to myself I'll never go near the community college again. I'll learn how to use a computer properly and go for a secretarial job like I used to have. But really, the picking up isn't all that bad. It's the vacuuming part that gets to me: the enormous rope of an extension cord, thicker than my leg, that I have to wind up and down the bleachers as I go and then eventually coil up again. Tantalus.

I'm thinking about a hot bath and some television. But when I get into the bathroom I find my skirt and blouse hanging on the towel rack and I remember: the poetry reading. I'm supposed to go with Christina to a poetry reading at the civic center, something Jace told her to do. It charms me that she wants me to come with her, and I'll take what I can get, even if it means being indirectly supportive of her boyfriend, who got her to tattoo lines from T.S. Eliot's "The Hollow Men" all over her arms.

I open the laundry chute and yell down, "Christina! Did you find your sweater?"

She seems to live in the basement. "Yah. Can you be ready to go in like fifteen minutes?"

"Uh huh."

I close the chute and get dressed. I gave up on makeup a long time ago but I hunt around for a lipstick. When Christina comes upstairs she's in black, as usual, but at least her tattoos are covered. "Yo, let's go," she says, twisting her dark hair with two fingers. "Jace will meet us there."

"Okay, okay," I say. "You drive. I can't stand your front seat driving."

We drive in silence. Christina swerves a little as we pull up to an intersection and she starts squeezing her right eye shut in a spasm.

"What the hell's wrong with you?" I say, reaching for the wheel.

"My contact, there's a fucking two-by-four in my eye," she yelps.

This is the melodrama of Christina. It must be God punishing me for all my childhood years of bursting into tears over busted dandelions or ants dying in kids' movies.

Christina parks the car as close to the handicap spots as possible. I'm thrilled that she doesn't park handicap, or in any other place that's inappropriate. She likes to wedge my car inside the cart racks at the Dominick's and climb out of the window and then, when she exits the store, act like she's shocked and outraged that somebody has built a cart rack around the car.

Christina's boyfriend waves at us from the door. He's scrawny, dressed in black like she is, but with his hair dyed white. "Hey, it's starting soon," he calls. He nods at me as we approach and then takes Christina's arm. "You read this poet before, Peter Sundahl?" he asks me.

I almost say, of course not, I'm way past the time when I enjoyed that kind of nonsense, but I smile and say, "No, but I'm open to the experience. Will he be selling his book tonight?"

"Yeah, when it's over," Jace says, squinting at me a little. I can tell he's onto me. He turns, still holding Christina, and I follow them into the auditorium. I understand that I am expected to sit apart from them and I settle into a chair in the row behind them. A girl hands us slips of paper: *Peter Sundahl Reading from his Newest Collection, "Polar Reversal."*

"Oh for God's sake," I mutter. The lights dim; there are about thirty other people in the auditorium when a tall and slender man moves down the center aisle and up the stage steps. He is silent as he arranges his books and his water bottle atop the podium in the middle of the stage.

I watch him. The stage lights catch a faint glow of blond in his otherwise graying hair, and when he looks up briefly, as though to acknowledge us, his brow is a little furrowed. He is probably in his late fifties. There is something about his hands, the way they move, that gets my attention: a gentle fluttering, a gracefulness in his long fingers and in the way he touches his temple as if to check his pulse. It is all very familiar, so much so that for a second I wonder whether I have met him before. He clears his throat. His voice is quiet and tentative: "Hello, good evening, I'm Peter Sundahl. I'm happy to be with you here, and I'll be reading from my collection . . ."

I don't hear the title or the first stanza of the poem he begins with. I find myself still staring at his hands. As he reads his right hand comes up and waves a little beside his head as though he is trying to figure something out. Then he stretches his fingers outward a little, gesturing to us. I think, again, that I must have known him before. And then, when he stammers just slightly, a soft "ah—" before he finds his place, I know who I am thinking of.

Christina never met her father, but he was like this, soft-spoken, with gentle hands and long, delicate bones. I met him on a train on my way into the city during the autumn of my second year at U of I. The car was packed, and I asked him very anxiously if I could sit with him. All the way to campus I stared at him, unable to stop myself; everything, the way he held his newspaper and the way he shifted in his seat, hurt me somehow, like I knew even then that I would love him and be hurt by it. When we got off at the same stop, I asked him his name. It was a confusing name—Mischael, not Michael—and mine was too: Francesca, which hadn't yet been shorn down to Fran.

He was studying the Russians—their languages, their literature and poetry. On the train the following morning he read to me from Pushkin. I still remember the scene he chose. It was in *Eugene Onegin*, where the girl goes into Onegin's abandoned study and looks at all his things spread out on the desk. She touches his writings and nearly goes mad with grief that she should be so close and yet so far from him, so hopeless at knowing him. I didn't know the story, but that was all I needed, and I think it was all Mischael needed, too, because his eyes were wet when we got off the train that second day.

I knew him for four months. Long enough to get to watch him make slits in tree bark and hide bits of verse inside, and long enough to follow him into the cornfields south of the city with his astronomy maps. He skipped class often. When he read something that moved him, he explained, he couldn't go sit at a desk. He would walk along the canal downtown and talk to people. He'd follow Lakeshore Drive to the stone steps behind Lincoln Park and let the waves soak his legs. Most of the time, I went with him.

I remember that a blizzard hit once while we were walking through the city, skipping class again, and that an old woman caught Mischael's arm and pulled him toward her. "Please," she said through the wind, "could you help me? I've lost my earring."

Mischael said something to her I couldn't quite hear and then, one hand still holding her arm, he crouched down and started peering into the snow that layered the walkway. I bent down beside him but could see nothing. Then Mischael plucked something up off the snow, and I saw that it was a pearl on his palm. He rose and pressed it into the woman's hand. "Here it is," he said, close to her ear. "Are you walking somewhere? Can I call you a cab?"

The woman assented, and Mischael went out into the street and flagged one down. He helped the woman into the taxi, said something to her, and then turned back toward me. His hair was sparkling with snow. When he took my hand he didn't look at me. In a distracted voice he said, "That is the first thing I've done in a year."

I didn't think too much about it until a month later when he said to me, in the middle of a completely different conversation, that he wasn't doing enough. "I have to do something," he told me. He was abruptly frantic, pacing around his room with his hands pressed to his temples. "I have to help somebody. Be better than this. Everything I do now, I do only for myself. This is all too easy."

I thought it was a phase he was in. He'd been talking about going into the ministry, maybe studying divinity. But then he told me he had accepted a volunteer position working with children overseas, in Korea, and I had to believe him. He left that spring. I never saw him again.

It all seems silly and sentimental now. Young man goes through moral crisis, launches himself into missionary work, abandons college career. What a crusader. How romantically selfless. But this poet in front of me with his gentle hands has me remembering Mischael's seriousness in a way I have been trying not to for seventeen years. After all, what good can it do me? My own story is as sappy and overdone as his. Young girl falls in love with crusader. Gives up virginity the night before he leaves for his mission. Gets pregnant and withdraws from the world, moves into underground apartment where illegitimate child is maladroitly raised. At thirty-seven has no prospects but can boast of years of saintly suffering. Gag me with a taffy apple.

It's actually easier for me to remember the bad years that followed Mischael's leaving—the years in that subterranean apartment in the city, where I left my toddler with a woman who lived above me so that I could support us. My Calvinist parents, who exiled me from the house, sent a small check every month that I assumed assuaged their consciences. There were nights when Christina and I both drank the formula I prepared in a plastic bottle. I grew up fast, quit crying over the Bronte sisters and classical music. Really, those first three years would have made a good movie, except that after all the sleepless nights and the bad food, I wasn't so pretty anymore, and Christina was anything but sweet. I swear she came out of the womb scowling.

"Fran."

I look up; Christina is turned around in her seat, hissing at me: "You have any chapstick?" I glance at the stage. Peter Sundahl is still speaking softly, his head bent a little over the podium.

"*Fran.*"

I fumble through my purse and hand it to her. In the low light, with her starkly-dyed hair and thick makeup downplayed, she looks pretty, even beautiful; she has her father's small mouth. I watch her put on the chapstick and then I take it back from her.

This whole setting isn't so bizarre for me to be in. I used to read poetry. I did that in high school, and with Mischael. Afterwards, when I was working to support Christina, I stopped doing things like that. The only thing I did that reminded me of him was stargazing. I had some of his maps and a pair of cheap binoculars. I used to take Christina outside and sit on our neighbor's stoop and pick out what pathetic number of stars I could locate in the Chicago-lit sky. Vega, Sirius, the obvious ones.

Transmissions

Even then, even in my early twenties living in a pit of an apartment with a baby, I found the time to be fascinated by space, the idea of life beyond our reach. I would think about what little I had picked up in science classes—theories about black holes, exploding stars, time warps—and just wonder and wonder about it. While Christina slept I would put the radio on low and when white noise came through I'd have a little shiver, and it wasn't a scared shiver, it was a lovely one, because I imagined that somebody was trying to communicate with me. Aliens occupying a world with violet rivers and yellow hills had singled me out for a few words.

Sometimes the truly ridiculous part of me imagined that Mischael, across the world, was sending out messages.

I quit thinking like that when Christina was two. I was cleaning the bathroom one night, and I had the baby monitor perched on the sink. She woke up and started talking to herself, little nonsense words that sounded like *moon mom moon mom*, and I sat back on my heels and just listened, and holding the bottle of ammonia in my hand I stayed there for a long time with my eyes closed. Her words: those were the transmissions I needed to be listening for. I had been a bad mother, I wasn't there enough. I put my radio on the curb in front of the apartment building and started reading to her at night, even after she'd gone asleep.

She didn't have a father until she was four, and that didn't last long either. I met Rob at my cousin's high school graduation party. Rob the Pug. It wasn't that he looked like a pug. He was actually a very good-looking man. He was just a little rough, had liked to get into fights at the pool halls when he was younger. He had been a state champion wrestler in high school and after that he coached. Some kid started calling him Pug behind his back, and it caught.

He was never violent with me or with Christina. He just decided when she was ten that he'd had enough of married life, of Christina's sassing back, of having to share his paycheck, of everything he'd gone almost thirty years not having to deal with. Actually, the real reason was probably the young woman who managed the wrestling team he coached, but I never got a confession out of him. I wasn't serious with anyone after that.

The sharp report of applause startles me. I look up again. The poet is still standing at his podium, and I feel truly guilty that I haven't heard a word of his work. It must be good. It seems like it would have to be, with the way he moves.

"Thank you all so much for listening," he is saying. "I would be happy to talk or answer questions with anyone who is interested in coming to the fellowship hall after this."

Christina turns around again as people start filing past us toward the door. "Jace and I are headed to his house," she says. Then, "Did you like it?"

I smile at her. "I did. I'm going to buy his book."

Jace twists around, too, and gives me an openly suspicious look. "Yeah right." But he breaks into a little grin. "You don't have to say that just for us."

"I'm not," I say, leaning forward. I mean it, too; I didn't hear a word but I intend to buy this man's book.

"Okay," Christina says, rolling her eyes. "We're heading out. See you later."

"What time will you be home?"

"By twelve?"

"Okay."

I watch them go. When they are out the door, I go and get a book from the table against the back wall. Then I follow the small crowd into the fellowship hall, where there is a long table set up with cookies, punch and plastic cups. The poet is standing at one end of the table, away from everyone, and no one is approaching him. I feel sorry for him and I wish he had something in his hands. Standing alone always seems easier when you have something to hold.

I pile some cookies onto a napkin, take my time pouring punch into a cup. As I sip at it I turn toward him and catch his eye.

It's a strange thing. He looks at me like he knows me; there's a softening in his face that is unmistakable. I look back down at the punch. I hope it's spiked, because my heart is actually pounding and I have no idea why I'm feeling like this, like I'm about to ask a man out on a date.

I peer at the poet again, over the cup. It occurs to me that this was how I got my first good look at Rob: over a glass, at that graduation party. I walked over to his table and introduced myself, and the sun was so bright I had to squint into his smiling face as I talked. I didn't know that a few years later I'd be donating my wedding gown to charity and searching through the newspapers for a one-story too far from Lake Michigan to be expensive.

But then there are those hands: he has them folded in front of him, and his chin is down a little as though conceding his invisibility. I put down my cup and cross the room to him. I'm not really conscious of maneuvering around people. It reminds me of when I was a little girl riding my bike—I'd be staring at something, a tree or a mailbox, and suddenly I was crashing into it, not knowing how I'd gotten there.

Peter Sundahl doesn't seem taken aback, though. He's holding out his hand, and his eyes, a soft blue, are crinkling a little at the corners.

"Thank you, uh, for your reading," I say. I'm about as good at socializing now as I was in high school.

"Thank you for coming to hear it. And you are—?"

"Francesca."

He is still shaking my hand, barely moving my arm. I want to turn around and see if people are behind me, waiting for him, but I tell myself to hold my ground. "I have to tell you, I really didn't hear any of your poetry tonight," I say. "Because your voice and the way you read just got me remembering things. I was just thinking the whole time. About the things I've missed."

"Maybe you did hear something, then," he says. "It seems like a lot of my poems are about that. The things I've missed. You looked like you were listening more than anyone else here."

"I did?"

"I'd say so." He nods at my book. "May I sign it for you?"

"I'd like that." I hand it to him, and he opens it to the inside cover.

I feel something curious happening as I stand in front of this man I don't know. Like the years are slipping off of me. I want to get lost in those eyes of his, hear his stories. There's a warmth, something to trust, in his face. He seems both older and younger than his years. I feel my own face changing, the muscles around my mouth softening, my eyes widening. I want him to tell me something. I want to receive something from this man, open myself to him. These are the kind of thoughts that I know will seem stupid, even perverse, later when I climb into my bed. But I can't stop them.

Peter Sundahl is watching me. He leans down a little and hands me back my book. He says, "Could I take you to dinner? I know this is probably very strange. I don't mean to be—I don't just ask, when I don't know somebody—but I'm wondering if you might like to? I'm in town until tomorrow morning."

I open my mouth to say yes. He is a lovely man, a good man, I can feel it in my bones. He might be twenty years older than I am, maybe more, but these things don't matter to me. I am aware that I could love this person and that it would be easy to do so.

I say, "When I said, the things I've missed? I wasn't talking about the things I didn't get to have. I was talking about the things I had for just a little while and then never had again. You know what I mean?"

He opens his mouth to answer, and a woman touches his elbow from behind. "Mr. Sundahl? Would you mind signing some books for us?"

He motions for me to wait before he turns around. I hover there for a moment and then start toward the door. Outside, the air is warm but dry and I breathe deeply. I get into my car and open the book. He's written, *to Francesca, so happily met in Chicago.*

I know something about love at first sight. I think it happens when a person's eyes or hands or voice suddenly forces you to take seriously all the things you try to make light of because they are just too beautiful, or too important. But I'm afraid to think about those things anymore, to imagine certain possibilities.

I start the car, turn on the radio. Static murmurs into the dark, and I can hear the faint hum of a distant voice. I go to put the car in reverse. Then the glass doors of the civic center open, and Peter Sundahl comes out, looking for me.

A Different Harbor

When Joanie and her parents find Joel at the Midway Airport, he's not in his uniform. He's dressed in a blue T-shirt and jeans and he has a massive duffel bag on his shoulder. Even without the uniform, though, he is easy to pick out: his cropped hair is palest blond, his skin drained of color, and he is twisting and un-twisting a newspaper between his hands.

Joanie's father pulls the van over and all three of them jump out. Joel has two days, just two, and they are overanxious, surrounding him. His mother crushes him to her, runs her hand over what little hair he has on his head; his father is talking fast, talking about getting dinner, a good shower, the friends who have called for him. Joanie, eight years old and too small for her age, stands on the curb looking up at her brother through thick glasses and gripping the end of his T-shirt in her fist.

It is Joanie who gets Joel's attention. She is too young to notice how detachedly he hugs his parents. What she knows is that her brother's familiar movement of dropping down to her eye level is happening again, and that his big pale hands are around her head. "Tot," he says sternly. "How goes it. Did you miss me?"

She looks into his face, at his pale lashes and wide, strong mouth. She notices that his eyes are red. "Yes. I collected a ton of things for you while you were gone."

"Oh yeah? Another caterpillar farm?"

"No, rocks and fossils."

Joanie's father raps Joel on the shoulder. "Let's get in the car, huh, before we get in trouble? I'll bet you want to get home and relax a little."

Joel shrugs and they climb into the van. All the way down 55 back toward Maywood, Joel is quiet, answering his parents' questions in monosyllables until his mother asks, "Aren't you happy to see home again?" Rapping his knuckles against the window, Joel says, "Oh yeah. The oasis that Maywood is."

Joanie barely catches the remark and doesn't quite understand. She is a child that rarely leaves the house. Vaguely she is aware that Maywood, with its tiny houses and police parked on every corner, is not a good place, but her world is the backyard and her bedroom, where she has boxes and jars and bottles filled with the things she collects.

Back at the house, Joel's father grabs the duffel, and his mother rubs him on the back as he starts toward the bathroom. "You have a hot shower, sweetheart," she murmurs. "I'll let you know when dinner's ready."

Joanie follows Joel to the bathroom door and hands him something: a blue cake of soap with a beach landscape carved into it. "I made this for you," she says.

"You little liar."

Joanie bursts into a guilty grin. "No, I didn't make it. But I got it for you."

He takes it, tries to smile back. He shuts the door harder than he meant to.

In the shower Joel mutters his mantra: "David Abrams, O Magnum Mysterium, South Haven."

It is a game he has been playing for four months, a game that started early one morning in the barracks when he was lying on his cot and realized he had no idea who he was anymore. They were rushing out at dawn and Joel knew he had just a few minutes more. The guy next to him woke up and started talking to Joel, but Joel couldn't hear a word he was saying because he was asking himself a question: if he had to pick out three things, three moments in his life that made him who he was, what would they be?

A Different Harbor

This was what he came up with. The first was David Abrams, a man he'd met in the city the summer after his high school graduation, when he was working in Chicago as a page. This guy was homeless and every day he sat on Canal Street, close to the bridge. He never shook a cup or called after anyone. On a Tuesday, Joel sat down next to the guy and asked him his name. This man Abrams told Joel that he had been homeless for eighteen months after losing his job at a paper mill. He had paper in his hands while he talked—he was trying to roll a cigarette with a chewing gum wrapper—and he told Joel that his two daughters lived in California and had no idea what had become of him. Joel was on lunch break, so he took Abrams to the Subway. Halfway through their lunch, he noticed something: their arms. They were almost exactly the same, if you took away the deep sunburn and the pockmarks on David's. After lunch Joel gave the guy the rest of what he had on him including his Walkman and then he went back to work. It was the first of many lunches he would have with Abrams.

The second thing Joel remembered was singing "O Magnum Mysterium" in the high school choir, at the winter concert his junior year. Really, it was singing itself that he remembered, but this particular song and the night they sang it seemed to encompass all the rest. There were less than twenty of them up on that stage, awash in light so bright that they couldn't see the faces of the audience, and they sang it in five-part harmony, Joel singing tenor. Something happened halfway through and Joel felt himself leave the ground. It was in the way their tones met at *beata virgo*, that tight bittersweet embrace of sound; it pained him; it was like lovers saying goodbye, a real and final goodbye, at a train station, the desperately intimate made public, and everyone could hear it yet nobody could know how it felt but Joel and the others creating those sounds, and then it was over and his eyes were wet and he had to close them.

The third thing was a place—South Haven, Michigan, where his family had gone on a little vacation about three years ago. They couldn't afford to go in summer and had to go in mid-autumn, and it was a miserable mistake; it was too cold to go anywhere, and they stayed in the hotel, watching the wind tear the beach apart. But on their last day, an unexpected snowstorm whirled down the coast—lake effect, they said—and Joel sneaked down to the hotel parking lot and got in his parents' van. He drove it to the harbor, battling the gales, and parked where he could see the lighthouse. At first it was only a faint pillar in the distance. But then, when the wind stilled, he saw it. Completely iced over, the lighthouse was a delicate spindle of ivory, and all along its rails, the blown waves had frozen in place like white wings suspended mid-flutter. It stunned him.

Lying in the barracks, it made him feel guilty and sad that this last thing, which he knew to be the most important, involved no person from his life. He had wondered before about his love for nature, whether it was misplaced, wrong somehow. It didn't seem like it should be. Nature seemed unselfish to him, always deflecting love and admiration away from itself and back to people or to God. Trees pointed upward; water mirrored the sky and rushed to shore. But still he felt guilty, and he reminded himself that the lighthouse he loved was not Nature, after all, but man, casting out light when disaster seemed imminent anyway.

"David Abrams, O Magnum—" He stops and shuts off the water, hearing a knock at the door that he knows is Joanie's. "Hold *on*," he says. With his fingers he rubs the landscape design off the top of the soap.

Returning to her room, Joanie sits down inside a circle of her collections and thinks about the Pretend Bugs. They were tiny glowing creatures she and Joel used to see in the empty spaces of the room after the lights went out. Their father told them it was static electricity but he didn't understand that these bugs did not operate on their own, but were completely at the mercy of Joel and Joanie's imagination, who made the bugs coalesce into shapes in the dark. Locomotives surging through the bedroom door. Scaly sea creatures surfacing at the foot of Joanie's bed. A dark house in the corner with a ghostly light in the window. The two of them went everywhere and saw everything with those bugs.

She wants to take Joel someplace other than this house but has a feeling he won't want to pretend anything. She considers the park. But the last time she was there, digging through the rocks and pebbles, a girl told her that she looked like a frog and that her elbows were dirty. She doesn't want to go back there.

Joanie picks up rocks. Pyrite, Galena, Turquoise. She knows most of their names. Petrified Wood, Moonstone, Lace Agate. The door opens, and Joel is standing there in the same clothes he had on before, impatiently running his hand over his head. "Do you have anything good to show me or what," he says.

Joanie jumps up. "Yes! This one I just got at the museum, when our class went. They had a bowl of them and you could pick any one."

She hands him a stone, a little polished chunk of pale green.

"What kind is this?"

"I don't know that one," she admits. "I can't always tell."

He sits down outside the circle and she starts showing him the other rocks, working her way down the line. For a moment, the old feeling comes back to her: she is Joanie May Benton, she knows the Periodic Table, she is important. She would not be afraid to go to the park and do whatever she wanted regardless of who else was there. It is what Joel with his calm, sure way has always done for her.

Years from now, after taking the Metra into Chicago, she will lose her timetable and panic when she can't find her train back home. An elderly conductor pacing alongside his train will see her and walk her all the way to where she needs to be. He will look almost exactly like an older Joel, with bright blue eyes and wisps of silvery blond just escaping his hat. She will befriend him, this older man, find out that he is unmarried and alone, and in befriending him she will find this feeling again.

Halfway around the circle of rocks, Joanie stops talking, a blunt arrowhead in her palm. Joel's eyes are on the window above her head, and he's dug a tiny hole in the carpet and buried a couple of the rocks in it.

"Hey," she says. "Are you still listening? What are you doing to my rocks? Look at this, it belonged to an Indian. It's from South Dakota."

Joel says, "Yeah, that's pretty cool, Joan," but he stands up fast, brushing off his pants like he's been sitting in dirt. "Let's go do something else, okay? You want to go outside?"

Their mother's voice cuts in: "Dinner, Joelie, Joanie." Joel suppresses a sigh. He can tell that she loves how their names sound alike, called out into the house.

Dinner is an agony, with Joel's father wanting to know exactly what he'd been doing out there and what he'll be doing next and Joel's mother talking too much about his health and the food he ate out there and then, worse, about what a man he has become, how proud she is. He doesn't eat much of the homemade fried chicken and macaroni.

Afterwards he goes down into the basement to look for some other clothes to wear. He roots through a Tupperware bin until he finds another tee and then starts back toward the stairs. Halfway there he notices a series of cardboard boxes lined up on the old picnic bench his mother uses for a laundry table. He peers into one of them. There are packages of toothbrushes inside. Maybe twenty packages. He lifts them and looks underneath. More toothbrushes.

The stairs creak. It is his mother. "Joelie? What are you doing?"

"Mom, what is all this?" He lifts up a package.

"They're for the Marines, honey. We send out boxes every month. Didn't I tell you that? They always need things like toothpaste and deodorant and—"

Joel is violently sorting through the next box, sending a couple packages to the floor. "Mom, this stuff has to get expensive. You can't keep on doing this."

She stares at him. Her light eyes are abruptly red-rimmed. "How could I not?"

"Well, don't."

She opens her mouth but says nothing.

"Just don't, for Christ's sake. Save your money. This is ridiculous."

"Joel!" Her hands are at her face; he knows it is his fault but he can't bring himself to move toward her.

"I'm sorry," he says at last. "I didn't mean it. Those guys—they need whatever you can send them. They always appreciate those packages when they come. Especially the good stuff, the candy."

"I always put candy in. Things that won't melt."

They walk back upstairs together, and just before they reach the top, Joel puts his hand on his mother's hair. This is what she will remember from today: toothbrushes, and that hand on the crown of her head.

Joel's father is in the kitchen. He is a tired-looking man in his late forties. He has kept the old Lou Malnati's together for ten years despite all the crime and vandalism the restaurant has endured. The family thinks of him as the wellspring of Joel's perpetual calm, but secretly Joel's father knows this to be a lie, that the truth is in fact the reverse, that he learned his calmness from his son.

Joel has seen his father in a panic only once. The two of them were working for the church, helping to tear down an old crack joint in the next town over. Joel's father, stripping beams on the second floor, stepped on a broken syringe that speared his shoe and broke the skin. Joel saw his father rush down the stairs, not favoring the leg, but sickly pale, crying out that he needed to leave and get to a doctor and could somebody please drive him. He had been terrified of an infection. AIDS, he'd told Joel later. Something that hibernates in you like an animal and then, when it's ready to come out, destroys you.

But the blood work had come back clean, and Joel never saw his father in a panic again. Now, sitting at the kitchen table, his father smiles at him. "Insane that they give you one lousy night, two lousy days," he says. "After all you've been through. You ought to get a paid vacation to, I don't know, one of those places with water you can see through to the bottom."

"Yeah, you'd think," Joel says, leaning over the kitchen counter. He pushes the handle on the toaster up and down, making a soft metallic screech. Joel hasn't told his father anything he has "been through." Nothing about the Strep throat that didn't ever go away or about the Jeep accident or about how it felt to pull a trigger and not be sure whether your bullet sank into somebody's body or not. These things, especially the last, have been happening to somebody else.

"You going to see any of your friends tonight?" his father continues. "Danny and Jordan called about a hundred times."

"No," Joel says. He releases the spring on the toaster and the pop is startlingly loud. "I think I might just take a drive. Can I use the van?"

"I guess so, sure."

"I want to take Joanie with me."

"This late?"

"I'll take care of her."

"Maybe you could just stay here? Your mother—"

"I said I'd take care of Joan, okay?"

"All right. What do I tell your friends?"

"That I'm tired. Or just don't answer the damn phone."

They look at each other, these two men, as though surprised, and Joel abruptly wishes that he could give his father a vacation to someplace with water you can see through to the bottom. A month from now, lying still inside an explosion of sound, he will find himself returning to this image, of all things: a glossy brochure lilting out of a mailbox, picturing a blue sea pierced with sunlight.

Joel finds Joanie arranging all of her rocks back on her dresser. "Will you come with me on a drive?"

She turns around, her eyes alight. "Of course. Where are we going?"

"You'll see. Get a jacket."

"It's not that cold out."

"It will be."

As they pass through the living room Joel's mother jumps up from the couch. "I don't know why you can't just stay here," she says. She puts a hand on Joanie's shoulder as if to keep her back, then looks at her. "I was going to make a cake."

When Joanie doesn't respond, her mother looks up at Joel, who only stares. "Okay," she says. "Okay. You be careful." She watches them go out the front door.

Joel swings the car out of the driveway so fast that Joanie scrambles to get her seatbelt buckled. On the road, it's clear that Joel doesn't want to talk. He flips the radio on and occasionally comments on how their parents need a new car. There is no map on his lap but he seems to know where he is going.

Twenty minutes pass, and Joanie sees that Joel's knuckles are white on the wheel. Her mind races for things to say that will make him smile. She reaches over and turns off the radio. "You want to play our own radio station?" she asks tentatively. It is a game they made up together when she was very young and they still shared a room. Joel would make up songs, and when she wanted a different one she'd say, "*Ch!*" into the darkness and he'd change the channel, switching to another song.

"You still remember that?"

"I remember some of the words from your songs. You sang the Ninja Turtles song sometimes but most of the other ones were made up."

"I hope you don't remember any of them. They must have been bad. How about we just put the real radio back on."

Joanie grins and her voice peals out high and theatrical: "*Oh my love, he is so handsome—*"

"Change that channel," Joel says.

Joanie giggles but her laughter dies out quickly and then silence descends again. She watches Joel, the hard line of his mouth. She wishes she had her rock collection, or something else to show him, even while he's driving the car, so that he will stop looking like this. But there's nothing in the van but some papers and a heap of old Sour Patch Kids in the glove compartment.

They are still on a wooded road, passing iron and stone gates that open into large estates set far back from the street. "Can you tell me what the place is?" Joanie asks, squinting through the trees.

"It's the water. Lake Michigan."

"Is it South Haven?"

"No. That's too far. This is a different harbor."

"Have I been there?"

"No, but I have. It's here in Illinois."

Joanie quiets. The minutes pass and she watches as the houses outside her window get smaller. They move out of the wealthy suburbs and into an area more like their hometown, only worse. There are beat-up cars parked in front yards, restaurants with signs that are barely legible, dimly-lit bars surrounded by weed gardens. The road is bad. Joanie says, "I don't like this." Joel says nothing, just stares at the road ahead.

They go over a series of potholes that send Joanie from one end of her seat to the other. They pass a sign that says ZION.

"Zion? Is that where the harbor is?"

"Almost."

A little further, and then Joanie spots a blue sign with white lettering that gleams under the streetlamps. WINTHROP HARBOR. She smiles at Joel but his white-lashed eyes are focused on the road. He curves the car right, down a narrow lane, and for a few minutes they drive through complete darkness.

Joanie's mouth falls open. A thousand orange lights have materialized outside her window. It takes a moment for her to realize that they are boat lights, that above them are the white masts of small crafts, pale and spindly like the skeletons of dandelions, and under them is a sheet of silken black water. The boats are barely moving, tied in for the night. In the distance is the vague outline of the marina. Joel drives toward it, and when Joanie turns to look at him, his eyes are fixed on the boat lights and she can see their orange glow in his face.

Joel parks the car as close to the harbor as he can get, in a little space marked *30 Minute Nonmember Parking*. The two of them climb out, and Joel comes around to take Joanie's hand. "Can we go down to the boats?" she asks.

Joel shakes his head. "Not us, we're not allowed there, but there's something better than that. It's a secret. C'mon."

She follows him to the other side of the marina, where at first all she sees are two bright, pulsating lights, one red and one green. Joel leads her down a gently-sloping hill of white rocks and sits her down with him. His hand rests on her shoulder. "See those lights?"

"Yes—?"

"Let your eyes focus. Wait."

Joanie stares. When her eyes adjust to the light, she realizes what she is seeing: two lighthouses, each at the end of a slender peninsula. The peninsulas stretch toward each other from opposite directions, and between them is a dark and glossy channel.

"Do you see the heat lightning? Way back behind the lights."

The lightning, a pale pink, illuminates heavy storm clouds in the distance, and in the flash of a moment, when it enflames the horizon line, Joanie can see the immensity of Lake Michigan behind the peninsulas. It is endless and black, and from it blossom the great clouds like a smoky mountain range. It all frightens her. She turns to her brother.

"You see, the boats go out through that little passage, between the lighthouses," he says quietly. His eyes are on the water. "They go through the passage, and then out to the real water. Sometimes they get caught in huge storms like the one that's going on way out there."

Joanie opens her mouth to ask, *do they always come back?* But she feels like she shouldn't be talking. Joel's hand on her shoulder is so tight it hurts.

They watch the lights. At last Joanie says, "Do you really have to leave again tomorrow?" Then, "Could we just pretend that you can go anywhere?"

Joel lets out his breath. "Anywhere you want, Joanie. We'll walk right across the water. We'll walk to Michigan."

About the Author

Elizabeth Genovise is a graduate of Hillsdale College in Michigan and of the MFA program at McNeese State University in southwest Louisiana. Her short fiction has been published in *The Southern Review, The Pinch, Relief, Yemassee, Pembroke Magazine, Cold Mountain Review, Driftwood Press, Labletter,* and other journals. Her next story collection, *Where There Are Two or More*, will be published in 2015 by Fomite Press. She hails from Villa Park, Illinois, and currently resides in east Tennessee.

Other Recent Titles from Mayapple Press:

Susana Case, *4 Rms w Vu*, 2014
> Paper, 72pp, $15.95 plus s&h
> ISBN 978-1-936419-39-5

Marjorie Stelmach, *Without Angels*, 2014
> Paper, 74pp, $15.95 plus s&h
> ISBN 978-1-936419-37-1

David Lunde, *The Grandson of Heinrich Schliemann & Other Truths and Fictions*, 2014
> Paper, 62pp, $14.95 plus s&h
> ISBN 978-1-936419-36-4

Eleanor Lerman, *Strange Life*, 2014
> Paper, 90pp, $15.95 plus s&h
> ISBN 978-1-936419-35-7

Sally Rosen Kindred, *Book of Asters*, 2014
> Paper, 74pp, $15.95 plus s&h
> ISBN 978-1-936419-34-0

Gretchen Primack, *Doris' Red Spaces*, 2014
> Paper, 74pp, $15.95 plus s&h
> ISBN 978-1-936419-33-3

Stephen Lewandowski, *Under Foot*, 2014
> Paper, 80pp, $15.95 plus s&h
> ISBN 978-1-936419-32-6

Hilma Contreras (Judith Kerman, Tr.), *Between Two Silences/ Entre Dos Silencios*, 2013
> Paper, 126pp, $16.95 plus s&h
> ISBN 978-1-936419-31-9

Helen Ruggieri & Linda Underhill, Eds., *Written on Water: Writings about the Allegheny River*, 2013
> Paper, 108pp, $19.95 plus s&h (includes Bonus CD)
> ISBN 978-1-936419-30-2

Don Cellini, *Candidates for sainthood and other sinners/ Aprendices de santo y otros pecadores*, 2013
> Paper, 62pp, $14.95 plus s&h
> ISBN 978-1-936419-29-6

Gerry LaFemina, *Notes for the Novice Ventriloquist*, 2013
> Paper, 78pp, $15.95 plus s&h
> ISBN 978-1-936419-28-9

Robert Haight, *Feeding Wild Birds*, 2013
> Paper, 82pp, $15.95 plus s&h
> ISBN 978-1-936419-27-2

For a complete catalog of Mayapple Press publications, please visit our website at *www.mayapplepress.com*. Books can be ordered direct from our website with secure on-line payment using PayPal, or by mail (check or money order). Or order through your local bookseller.